## Chapter 1

Danielle Cooper glanced over the top of her computer monitor. He was walking through the open plan office, and towards the main meeting room. She really did not understand what all the fuss was about.

What a prick, she thought.

Josh Linberg was arrogant and egotistical. Even the way he walked irked her. He had a swagger that was entirely manufactured for the sole purpose of attracting maximum attention.

He was relatively tall, she would guess a few inches over six feet. As a professional athlete, he was lean and muscular. His body shape was A typical for a twenty-eight-year-old footballer.

He was dressed in a navy-blue cotton sweatshirt and matching sweatpants. The JL13 logo was proudly stitched on the left breast, and right upper thigh of his ensemble. He wore a pair of crisp white designer trainers, the colour of which matched perfectly complementing, and accentuating the logo. She'd put him at a size eleven shoe, and wondered whether the large feet were representative of other sizeable areas.

He was tanned from his recent trip to Dubai. He had been over there for three weeks to attend an end of season training camp. Danielle thought she could see the faint tan lines you get from wearing sunglasses in the hot weather. The subtly paler skin around his eyes, and across the bridge of his well-defined nose, further highlighted the vivid forest green eyes he had.

He did have nice eyes. That she would concede. He had long lashes too, and she liked that. What she didn't like, was men who waxed their eyebrows. She would put money on him waxing his legs too. He had a well-defined jawline that would suit a beard, though she wasn't sure he was able to grow one. Danielle loved a bit of stubble on a man.

If further evidence was needed to demonstrate his love for himself, he wore some form of visible lip balm.

Yep, he was a man who had shiny lips!

His hair was styled perfectly. Parting slightly off centre, his bleached blonde locks hung down each side of his face, and framed his tanned forehead. He reminded Danielle of Nick Carter from the Backstreet Boys. When she had pointed this out to Ginny, she was met with a confused look, immediately making Danielle feel old.

1

'Look it up,' she had told her.

Danielle knew she was in the minority. The women in the office practically swooned whenever he was around. He often winked in the general direction of one of the more attractive in the bunch. This guaranteed the topic of water cooler gossip for at least the rest of the week.

'Did you see him wink at me?' she would overhear one gloating to the others, when she passed them huddled around the reception desk.

He may as well have had 'fuck boy' tattooed on his forehead. He knew the effect he had on women, well, some women. He seemed to enjoy the reactions resulting from one of his winks, or his trademark smiles. He certainly lived up to the reputation represented in the tabloids.

Danielle had seen many a headline depicting a lady's' man. The accompanying pictures would lead the reader to believe he was single, even though he was not. Last year, he had posted a video to his social media accounts, making a public apology to his long-term girlfriend. It must have done the trick because she was still with him!

His legions of fans did not seem to care. Hell, all the females in the office adored him. How could they

2

be so naive? One wink and they were picking out bridesmaid dresses, and drafting the celebrity guest list for the impending nuptials.

Danielle had nicknamed him, 'Mr Smarm'.

She preferred her men dark and rugged. She liked a bit of chest hair, as long as it was well maintained. She doubted very much that Josh was able to *grow* chest hair.

Whatever Danielle thought about Josh's Lothario antics, he had been surprisingly involved and hands on with the work. JL13 was his brainchild, and he had been heavily influential in setting the agenda for the brand. Unlike many celebrities who have designers and creatives employed to do the grunt work, Josh could proudly sign his name to authenticate the merchandise.

Josh was now in the meeting room at the head of the table. She could see his outline through the frosted glass. He was leaning back in the chair, already losing interest in the finance director, who was speaking to the occupants animatedly.

Considering his occupation, money wasn't anything Josh was going to sweat over.

She dropped her gaze back to her screen. It was black. She wiggled her mouse, realising she had clearly looked longer than intended. The monitor instantly came back to life, and her home screen flashed a picture of her beautiful nephew, Taylor. He was smiling at the camera, dressed in his full West Ham kit.

Taylor loved West Ham. LOVED them! Her whole family did. She had grown up in a house with a dad and two brothers who were season ticket holders. Now retired, her dad followed his team around the continent to watch them play. It was no surprise Taylor was now the next generation of Cooper, and carrying the mantle. Danielle was pretty sure he would be disowned if he supported another team.

Luckily, Taylor, although only six, was a die-hard Hammer. When Danielle told him her next project was working with Josh Linberg, he was frantic with excitement. Josh was his favourite player. Danielle had earned the title of 'favourite auntie', for at least the next few months. A fact that she wasted no time in teasing her little sister with.

She and her sister would often compete for the title of best auntie. Their mother would chastise them when they playfully argued over the crowning honour. 'He loves you both equally', she would say. They knew that really.

## Chapter 2

The time displayed in the bottom right-hand corner of her screen said two forty-five pm. She hadn't realised lunchtime had come and gone, but that wasn't unusual. Danielle often forgot about food until her stomach growled at such an audible level, Ginny would march over to her desk and attempt to convince her it was time to eat.

Ginny was good like that. It had taken some time for the two of them to establish a working relationship, but now that they had, Ginny was an invaluable asset.

Danielle didn't know exactly why, but other women didn't like her much. It had always been that way for as long as she could remember. As early as high school, she had been shunned by the girls. It wasn't something that really bothered her. She had a tight knit group of friends that she had known forever. They were the only people, aside from her family, who really knew her. She had a fair few acquaintances and work colleagues, and she enjoyed the occasional drink with them, but she never revealed her true self, not really.

She learned very quickly that making friends at work could lead to disaster. Fresh out of college, Danielle's first job was in the office of an accounting firm. She made tea, typed up notes and collected files for anyone that asked. She did not know anyone when she joined, and was thrilled when Laura had befriended her. Laura was a personal assistant to the senior partner in the firm. Before long, she had asked Danielle to join her for a drink. Happy to be making friends, she agreed, and they headed to a quaint little wine bar hastily, the minute the workday had ended.

When they sat down, drinks in hand, Laura moaned about the work being tedious and her boss being handsy. Danielle joined in. She told Laura how mind numbingly boring the role was, and that she thought that a junior partner was having an affair with the young girl that did the payroll. Danielle recounted the time she had entered the file room and found them in an embrace. Payroll girl, Danielle couldn't remember her name, quickly picked up a file, and scurried out of the room, red faced. They sat for the rest of the night exchanging stories and getting progressively more drunk.

When she went to work the following day, she was called in to the office and chastised for speaking out of turn. She was put on probation and, to add insult to injury, the payroll girl 'accidentally' underpaid her in the next months' pay packet. She quit that job and told them to stick it, but she had learned a valuable lesson. Well, a couple actually.

Firstly, she learned that there was a time and a place for pure honesty, and it was not to work peers. Secondly, she should not automatically assume that all people are genuine, and can be taken at face value. From that point forward, she would assume the worst and protect herself.

After the incident at the accounting firm, she abided by her newly imposed rules when at work. Danielle knew that she may sound cynical. She wasn't bitter, she was grateful for the life lesson. It didn't mean that she would be unapproachable. She was more than happy to exchange pleasantries, and go out for lunches and drinks. She just limited these encounters to the working week, and didn't discuss work matters with colleagues outside office hours. At the weekend, she only surrounded herself with her oldest friends and her family.

She did enjoy working with Ginny. Unlike the girls in reception, Ginny was straight talking and wasn't interested in bullshit. She was a natural beauty. She had blonde hair that she usually wore in a ponytail, and a thick blunt fringe. She didn't wear makeup other than a little mascara. The inky black liquid highlighted her piercing blue eyes, which were permanently framed with black rimmed Donna Karen specs.

Ginny was always perfectly turned out. Her office wear was professional and stylish. Danielle was quite envious of her ability to create a look from individual pieces, she would never have thought to put together. Her petite frame could pull off any outfit. Danielle herself, stuck to traditional work attire. Usually, some form of A-line dress, tights, and heels.

Ginny had a face full of sweet and subtle freckles that gave her the look of a timid schoolgirl. Her five-foot stature only added to the illusion. In reality, it couldn't be further from the truth. A bookish schoolgirl was not Ginny at all. Danielle had seen her slutdrop seductively, and play tonsil tennis, with more than one stranger on the dance floor in the three months she had been working at JL13.

As a freelance project manager, Danielle did not have a permanent place of work. She moved from office to office, based on the project she was working on at the time.  Danielle worked mainly with start-ups. Either new companies entirely, or organisations that were diversifying into other markets.

Her role was to bring together all the individual stakeholders, and develop a cohesive strategy to launch. She was strong minded, analytical and logical. These character traits made her extremely good at her job.

She had been employed in this role before for a single company. There, she found the red tape and internal politics stifling and counterproductive. Starting her own business afforded her autonomy, and the freedom to choose which projects she took on. Being an external party, she had no affiliation with any one department. She didn't have to tip toe around a contentious issue, or placate any department heads.

Her style was not for everyone. She made a point of outlining the way she worked with potential clients before agreeing to come on board. She appreciated that some business models were not compatible with her no-nonsense approach. She didn't take it personally. After ten years of building up her network, she had amassed a portfolio of admirable testimonial's. Now, her reputation bought clients to her, without the need for her to advertise her services. She had a website, but that was used by potential clients to make initial contact.

Word of mouth was how she landed this role. She got a call from Lucy Turner who was the newly appointed managing director of JL13. Danielle had worked with Lucy previously on a start-up. Lucy had spent weeks trying to secure Danielle. She was initially reluctant, as a clothing line was quite different from her usual sector. Eventually, after some negotiation, she agreed to come on board. After all, it didn't actually matter what the product was, her role was to make sure it got over the line effectively and efficiently.

JL13 was a sports and loungewear clothing line. The concept was affordable clothing for men and boys. It's unique selling point was the patented fabric used to make the clothing was durable. It maintained shape and colour vibrancy through multiple washes, therefore making it perfect for sports enthusiasts, who regularly got dirty in pursuit of their hobby.

It was the longest project she had agreed to work on. Three to six months was the average but here, she had agreed to a twelve-month term. Danielle had insisted that if she were to take on the project, she would need time to research the market.

Josh was the brand. It was his initials and shirt number that titled the company, and adorned every piece in the collection. A sportsman promoting a sports and loungewear brand had great synergy. A sportsman of Josh's calibre ensured a slam dunk. Success was all but certain, the challenge for Danielle was to get it over the line. His schedule was mapped out for most of the year with footballing commitments. This meant that there was only a very tight window he could commit himself to.

Josh had created some rumblings in the press by wearing a selection of the merchandise in public. This was by design and had the desired effect. The launch was now imminent. Sign off from Mr Smarm was the last item on the agenda, and hopefully today would be the day!

## Chapter 3

'Ginny, could you please do a final proofread of the presentation, and pack information, whilst I pop to the ladies?' Danielle asked.

She pushed back on her cream leather swivel chair, smoothing her navy pinstriped knee length dress down. Danielle was already sold on affordable clothing. She didn't like to spend exorbitant amounts of money on work attire. She had the means to, but begrudged parting with her hard-earned cash, for the same material and manufacturing process used by both Prada, and the main high street brands. She still managed to look the part.

'Sure thing Dan,' Ginny answered.

'If you're one hundred percent confident that there are no spelling or formatting errors, you can print the packs. Do nine just in case,' Danielle called back to Ginny, as she was heading to the bathroom.

She didn't hear an answer, but knew Ginny had heard her and would do as she had asked.

Danielle was washing her hands in the ladies bathroom. The sweet smell of the floral Jo Malone hand gel was intoxicating. She looked up from the basin and into the circular mirror in front of her. Rinsing absentmindedly under the warm water, she inspected her face, making sure her makeup was still set. She had noticed the last few nights when removing her makeup, black smears under her eyes from rubbing them.

Danielle could admit, if only to herself, that she had been feeling the effects of the sixteen-hour workdays in the last week. She was so ready to get this final meeting done, and the launch underway.

She took a step back from the basin, unravelling and drying her hands with a white cotton cloth. The cloths were neatly stacked in a wicker basket on the countertop. She looked in the full-length mirror mounted on the wall to her right. As a size sixteen, Danielle knew that she was on the larger side. She was curvaceous. Her thighs were thick, and her stomach was not entirely flat. There were lumps and she was ok with that.

As far as Danielle was concerned, it was better to enjoy the food she ate, rather than to live off lettuce leaves and be miserable. She would most definitely be miserable if she lived off salad. Not that she disliked it, she just did not want to eat it every day.

She was comfortable with the way she looked. She knew that being a bigger girl, she would not be attractive to some men, and that was fine with her. Any man that was put off by a little wobble here and there, was not the type she would want to spend her time with anyway. Danielle didn't find herself lacking in male attention. She was confident in her own skin, and found that men were attracted to that.

She had tried all different diets and exercise regimes when she was in her twenties. Nothing had worked. Back then, she was the same as any other twenty something. Hoodwinked in to thinking that beauty was the airbrushed images of celebrities and reality tv stars, with washboard stomachs and tiny frames. Danielle would spend hours looking at herself in the mirror, pulling and poking at the bits of her body she didn't like. She would often cry after stepping on her scales, having not lost a pound after a week of intense, borderline starvation methods.

It was only after she left her mum and dad's house that she had regular access to scales. When she lived at home, her mother refused to keep them in the house. She would tell her and her sister that women come in all shapes and sizes. That they would know if they gained weight by the tightening of their clothes.

Danielle always felt she was attractive. When she reached thirty, she realised that the self-torture was not worth the hassle. Reluctantly, she conceded that her mum was right, not that she would admit it to her.

She began to own her figure and wear it with pride. She switched her efforts to being healthy and happy. Danielle's weight stabilised, and she grew a confidence she had previously never thought possible.

Her hands dried, she threw the used cloth in to the bin under the sink. She turned to the side, looking at her reflection from that angle. As she trailed a hand over her stomach, she heard a flush, the click of a lock being slid across, and the door of the other toilet cubicle open.

Danielle smiled at the woman who emerged. She was still fastening the belt that sat very neatly round her extremely tiny waist. Her white, blonde hair framed her horse-like face, and cascaded down her back, finishing slightly above the belt she had just finished fastening. The belt pulled her in at the waist, and accentuated her large breasts. They were disproportionate to her small size and frame.

Danielle thought it was highly likely their enhanced size may not be a genetic anomaly. Her obviously artificially filled plump lips curled into a fake smile in response. The girl quickly shuffled out of the door, and headed back toward her desk.

'Dirty bitch didn't wash her hands,' Danielle muttered under her breath.

Alone in the bathroom, she took one last look at herself in the mirror, smiled, and exited ready to collect Ginny and her laptop for the meeting with Mr Smarm.

## Chapter 4

The JL13 office meeting room looked pretty much the same as any other she had presented in. Floor to ceiling glass formed three of the four walls, with the fourth being taken up by a large screen set on a beige painted wall. The bottom half of the glass walls were coated with whatever they used to blur out, but not entirely camouflage the interior of the room from outsiders.

Danielle never understood this. Meetings by nature were private affairs. That is why they were held in a separate room, and the door was usually closed when in session. Having half the room shielded didn't prevent everyone outside from looking in. The occupants' heads and faces were still visible. This was surely what you would want to shield from any prying eyes, or eager lip readers?

In the corner of the space was a white board resting on an easel. The only time Danielle had ever seen the whiteboard used, was as a resting place for a flipchart. The main floor space in the room was taken up by a gargantuan mahogany topped table. Surrounding the table, were twelve identical cream backed leather chairs, not at all dissimilar to Danielle's own desk chair.

As Danielle entered the room, she felt a pang of hunger, and cursed herself for not grabbing an apple from the fruit bowl in reception. She hoped to God the audible growl that usually followed, would not be loud enough to attract the attention of the attendees, already seated at the table.

She took her seat as Ginny went round the table handing a pack to everyone. This meeting included all the department heads whose sign off was required to move forward. From left to right the attendees were as follows; Lucy Turner, Managing Director, Dave Barker, Marketing Director, Jarrod Smith, Head of Ecommerce and Website Creation, Audrey Roberts, Content Creator, Josh Linberg, CEO, Corrin Bailey, Advertising Director and Press Liaison, and Ginny, Senior Business Analyst and Strategist. Collectively, these people were instrumental in delivering the launch of JL13.

As with most small companies, there was a constant undercurrent of each employee fighting for pole position. Danielle was careful to be sensitive of this, but sometimes it was infuriating. In order to include everyone equally, each department head had been assigned an area to own. Danielle has implemented a daily meeting to allow everyone to share their progress, and ensure the cohesive strategy was adhered to. Josh did not attend these meetings. She wanted him to provide sign off once all the smaller details had been ironed out.

The meeting today was to do just that. They each had a section of the slide deck to present. Danielle would bring it all together by demonstrating the timeline assigned to each element of the day's itinerary. Josh wasn't attending blind. He had been involved in the initial creation of the timeline, and had specified the requirements essential to his vision. She was confident that all areas were meticulously set, and every individual knew what they were bringing to the table.

Grabbing the port from the middle of the table, Danielle plugged it in to the back of her laptop.

'Why do we have paper as well as the screen presentation?' Josh asked.

'I find it helpful to follow the screen presentation with the pack so that any notes taken have a reference point,' Danielle responded.

She tapped a key on her laptop, typed in her password, and her home screen was duplicated on the wall mounted tv. All the occupants of the room had quietened. They were briefly looking at Taylor's cute little face, then she loaded the PowerPoint document, ready to begin.

Josh was yet to sit up straight. Danielle found this quite rude, but didn't allow that to show on her face. No sooner had she thought this, he leaned forward in his chair, and picked up his copy of the pack.

'I'll need a pen then so I can take notes,' he said, standing up and making his way to the now closed meeting room door.

He smiled and winked at Dave, who was trying and failing to supress a laugh. A snort escaped him as he winked back at Josh. The exchange made Danielle's face redden slightly with anger. She knew exactly what all that was about. Josh was going to go and get himself a pen from reception, taking full advantage of another reason to flirt.

Danielle knew that Josh had a girlfriend. He had told her so when they first met. He had a framed picture of them at the beach on his desk. So why was he blatantly flirting with other women? That wasn't Danielle's problem she decided. She, and everyone else were now sat waiting for him to return.

Moments later he did so, pink fluffy pen in hand. He couldn't have just gone to the stationary cupboard and got a standard biro? Danielle rolled her eyes.

'I'm readddy,' he said, with subtle sarcasm.

He retook his seat and made a point of holding the pen poised for note taking. She responded by flashing him her best 'eat shit' smile, and began her presentation.

'That went well I thought,' Ginny said, as they sat back down at their desks.

It did go well. Apart from Dave querying something just to amuse Josh, and attempt to knock her off her stride, all was signed off.

'Wanna go for a quick drink to celebrate? I think we've earned it don't you?' Ginny asked.

'I could go for one,' Danielle said. 'Let's get out of here'.

She hadn't bothered to re-open her laptop. She just packed it away in her Hermes tote, and headed past the now empty reception, and straight for the elevator. Unlike her aversion to expensive clothing, Danielle was not opposed to spending a decent amount of money on a bag. With a bag, she could confidently say there was a marked difference in quality. A good bag could last a couple of years and, considering it was used frequently, that was a sensible investment.

Bags, shoes and jewellery. Those were her indulgences.

The JL13 office was not situated in a typical area of London for a fashion brand. Josh and his primary team decided to rent office space whilst they were creating the first seasons look. The plan was to move into permanent premises, after the first products hit the market.

Josh's' dad played golf with someone who owned a property in Leadenhall Street. His former tenant had vacated, at the same time they were looking for space.

Danielle was surprised when she arrived at the office for the first time. Leadenhall street was in an area synonymous with insurance companies. Their building was almost exactly opposite Lloyd's of London. The general area was familiar to Danielle as she had worked on a few insurance projects. A clothing brand in this area would stick out like a sore thumb. Or she supposed, it could do the exact opposite.

When Josh started working on the project, it was top secret. If he had secured offices near or around the likes of Nike and Adidas, his presence in that area would attract unwanted attention. In this area, even if he was recognised, everyone was far too busy, and self-absorbed to pay him any mind.

And so, they occupied the fifth of six floors inside the non-descript old office block. Most of the other levels were rented as a glorified mailbox for businesses that wanted to have an EC3 post code. These floors were mostly empty. The businesses needed more floor space to house their staff. They therefore occupied much cheaper offices outside of the city.

There was an old commercial fleet brokerage on the first floor. Their staff totalled ten, and they averaged an age of sixty. All of them were sweet older gentlemen who were usually back home by lunchtime. Danielle often saw one or two of them holding manilla folders under their arms, and heading towards Lloyd's. She imagined they had been in business for close to forty years, and now had just a small number of loyal clients to maintain.

The world had changed so drastically since their glory days. She thought it would be really interesting to listen to their stories. She recalled an old colleague of hers telling her that business was done in the pub on the back of a cigarette packet, when they were four bottles of red wine deep. The governing bodies had put a stop to that kind of activity long ago. Taking a client out to lunch these days had to be carefully considered. Business outings needed to be justified to ensure they couldn't be judged as coercion.

The lift doors opened on the ground floor, and Ginny and Danielle stepped out into the run down and dingy foyer.

'Goodnight Gladys,' Ginny said as they walked past the main reception desk, and the lone receptionist. She was eyeing them with interest.

Gladys looked at her watch and said, 'Six forty-five ladies? That's the earliest I have seen you leave for a while.'

'We are celebrating the end of the extremely late nights,' Ginny said, linking her arm through Danielle's.

'Enjoy. Have one for me won't you,' Gladys said.

'We'll have four for you,' said Danielle, as she unhooked her arm from Ginny's to push the revolving door, out into the warm evening.

## Chapter 5

'Rooftop or dive bar?' Asked Ginny. She retook her position at the side of Danielle, with her arm looping again.

'Rooftop in this weather I think,' Danielle responded.

She looked up into the evening sky and noticed the sun was already lowering. Surrounded by tall buildings and skyscrapers, the lowering of the sun had no impact on the heat on the street. Danielle did not know what it was about London, but it always seemed to be unbearably hot in the summer months. Her dad had told her that the heat got trapped in by the compact layout of buildings, and had no space to escape. She wasn't sure, but her dad was an architect, so she supposed he knew what he was talking about.

Hot or not, Danielle was in awe of this city. The juxtaposition of the Monument, two roads away from the new age glass giant that was the 'gherkin' building. The 'walkie talkie' building, a short walk from the great Tower of London. A Capital city that was richly saturated in world famous history dating back to the Roman Empire. Evidence of a world that could no longer be fathomed at every turn. Modern industry and enriched history unlikely companions, and yet somehow coinciding in imperfect harmony.

Ginny and Danielle walked through the glass doors of the Hilton Doubletree on Pepys Street, and were instantly met with the cool air-conditioned foyer.

'That feels so good,' Danielle said.

She slowed her pace considerably, to savour the reprieve from the close and repressive weather outside. They walked past the reception desk where two perfectly preened members of staff were checking in the over nighters, and took a right heading for the elevators. Danielle pressed her room key against the reader to call the elevator to the ground floor. It arrived almost immediately, and they stepped in to the car. Danielle pressed the buttons for the seventh and twelfth floors.

'I'm thinking espresso martinis.' Ginny sang in a high-pitched voice. She was looking at Danielle's reflection in the lift mirror as they ascended.

'I need to put my laptop in my room, and I'll meet you there,' Danielle said. She thrust her corporate card into Ginny's hand.

'Drinks are on Mr Smarm tonight,' Danielle said.

Ginny's grin widened as she eyed the platinum American Express card with eager delight. Danielle stepped out and on to the seventh-floor corridor making the short walk to her room. She slotted her key card in the reader on the door handle, and waited for the light to flash green, granting her access.

Her executive suite was not too shabby at all. The room boasted a super king size bed. It was dressed in white linen Egyptian cotton sheets, expertly pressed with no creases in sight. Danielle wondered whether the maids had specific training before being allowed to maintain the super king beds. Doing so was most certainly a skill. She knew without doubt, she could never achieve the smooth and taut finish left for her every evening.

Not wanting to chance ruining the sheets, Danielle set her laptop and charger on the low coffee table next to the bed. She turned, and left the room, eager to taste the sharp sweet deliciousness that was the Hilton espresso martini.

After calling the elevator, she stepped through the open doors sending a quick message to her mum. She let her know she was out for the evening, and she would therefore call her tomorrow. Her gaze pointing down at the screen as she typed, Danielle was in her own world when she walked into the person who was already in the car.

'So sorry,' she said, looking up from her phone apologising to the man.

She glanced up at the hat wearing stranger she had just assaulted, and was startled to see piercing green eyes staring back at her. His lips thinned in an attempt to suppress a smile, causing the corners of his mouth to twitch.

'No worries Danielle,' Mr Smarm said.

He took a step back and leaned against the rail support. She didn't know what to say next. She was so surprised to see him there, her head was a bit scrambled.

'You, what are you doing here?' she asked, the words spilling out of her unexpectedly.

'I'm staying in the hotel if that's alright with you?' he said, not taking his eyes off her.

Danielle thought his words sounded challenging, almost menacing. It was as if he was trying to goad her into a response.

'Me too,' she said, and threw him an obviously fake smile, not taking the bait.

She wondered if he already knew that. Surely, he could not have been aware she was residing in the same hotel, or else he would have booked another. She hadn't bumped into him in the three months she had stayed here. Then again, she supposed that he probably didn't book the hotels he stayed in himself, he would have someone to do that for him.

'Which floor?' he asked.

'Twelve,' she responded. He pressed the corresponding button.

'Me too,' he said, 'I'm meeting Dave for a pint'.

Danielle rested her back against the handrail. Mildly annoyed that they were drinking in the same bar, they rode the elevator in awkward silence.

Josh was twenty-eight and therefore moving toward the back end of his professional football career. The majority of players hung up their boots not long after reaching their early thirties. That was unless you were extremely disciplined, and treated your body like a temple. This meant no alcohol, and a healthy diet, three hundred and sixty days of the year.

Danielle had learned this during her research phase of the project. She had read that Christiano Ronaldo was almost forty, and still had a regular spot in his team squad, as well as representing Portugal at international level. He, and a small few others had broken the mould, but they were the minority. If Josh was planning to have a pint ten days before the start of the new season, he was almost definitely not following in the footsteps of Ronaldo.

He was in good shape though, Danielle had to admit. He wore a relatively loose-fitting tracksuit, but she could see the outline of his pecks. His thighs were huge and tight. She bet that if she touched them, they would be hard as stone, even if he was not flexing them.

The noise of the elevator dinged, and the robotic female voice announced, 'level twelve'. This made her jump, and shocked her back into the present.

'Have a nice evening,' she said.

She bolted through the open doors, and made a beeline for the terrace. She was eager to get to the sweet, sweet espresso martini that should be waiting for her.

## Chapter 6

'Danielle, over here,' a voice called through the crowd of businessmen and women.

The voice did not belong to Ginny. She headed towards the call, and found the owner of that voice sitting in the VIP area. The man's left arm flew up to wave her over, whilst his right was draped over the back of the plush garden sofa, and looking suspiciously close to Ginny.

'Fancy bumping into you,' Dave said, as Danielle took a seat in the chair opposite.

They were separated by a low set fire pit encased in thick glass edging. Obviously not alight on a balmy evening like this, the five inch white marble rim that surrounded the pit, served as an excellent table to set down a drink. Talking of drink, Danielle looked around for hers and quickly located it in Dave's dumpy little hand.

'Sorry, not sorry,' he said, as he registered her eyeing the near empty glass.

Bloody hell she thought. She had only been gone for ten minutes, and that included the time it took for Ginny to order, and the barman to make the damn drink. She rose from her seat, choosing not to respond. She was intending to order a double round, when she felt a hand on her shoulder, preventing her from reaching full height. The hand gently pushed her back down to her seat.

'J bone,' Dave shouted. He set the empty glass down and opened his arms in a welcoming gesture.

'Can you not draw attention this way for fuck's sake. I thought we were having a pint not a cocktail?' he paused a moment. 'Same again?' Josh finished. He was looking down at a now reseated Danielle.

'I was going to get them,' she said in response.
'Probably best I do as I am assuming, by the addition of the hat, you are choosing to go incognito this evening?'.

'I am,' he said, 'thought I could get away with it too, until this one shouted,' nodding towards Dave.

'Probably shouldn't have worn a tracksuit that displays your initials and shirt number,' Danielle pointed out. She rose from her seat again to go to the bar.

He caught her arm this time when she had almost passed him. His grip was a lot less gentle as he pulled her back towards her seat. She looked from his hand still on her arm, then up to his face, ignoring the jolt that shot through her when he grabbed her.

'I might not want to be recognised by anyone else, but I did catch the eye of this fine lady, and she has dedicated the rest of her shift to attending to my every need.'

Danielle yanked her arm away from his grip. She followed his shit eating grin to the busty brown-haired waitress in the low-cut top.

'Jessica darling,' he said. He took a step closer to her, knowing the effect it would have. 'Could we please have four more espresso martini's and four pints of your finest Amstel?'

'Yes of course Sir,' she said. She stared at him a little longer than was necessary. Eventually, she broke the stare and headed for the bar.

As Josh sat down in the solo seat next to Danielle, he laughed. He winked at Dave who was displaying a look of utter admiration, and twitching as if he didn't know whether to clap, or hug him.

Dave was envious. Danielle was sure he must be in his mid-forties, and well past his prime. The waist band of his trousers gave away the fact he had put on weight.

34

What was previously a well-fitting suit, now shoddy and bursting at the seams. He wasn't fat, but he had clearly chosen to ignore the fact that he had widened since he purchased his attire. His cheeks were permanently red, betraying that he either had high blood pressure, or a bit of a drinking problem. Maybe both.

Despite this, his face was kind. He had bags under his eyes from the long workdays, and busy family life. He had a couple of children Danielle remembered. He had told her that the youngest hadn't slept through the night since they brought her home from the hospital. She was now five.

His hair was a mousy brown, and she could see evidence of his age and stress by the flecks of grey hair near his temple, and in his sideburns. She had gotten to know him in the last few months and her original opinion of him had changed. Though she didn't agree with some of his habits, she knew that the garish ties and socks he wore, did not reflect who he was at home. At work, he was loud and obnoxious.

He played up to the 'geezer' stereotype. Danielle felt that he acted this way because he thought that was what made him likeable. This was never more evident than when Josh was around. Any feeling of warmth she may have felt when Josh held her arm abated, and was quickly replaced by a feeling of annoyance. Ginny had sat silently taking in this whole exchange with interest. No emotion registered on her face, though Danielle was sure she had kept her eyes on her a beat longer than needed.

'So,' Ginny said, 'I assume you two are staying with us?'

'If that's ok with you ladies?' Josh answered her, but pointed the question at Danielle.

'Of course it is,' Ginny replied quickly, before Danielle had a chance to form any words herself.

'Right then Ginny, let us have an update on your dating life,' Josh said. 'I am eager to get more info following the dalliance with Christoff the croupier'.

Danielle was slightly taken aback, though she thought she had got away without showing it. She didn't know Ginny and Josh were that friendly. She wondered if they... no! Ginny would have told her surely? Danielle pushed that thought away and pulled her chair in closer. She was as eager as the others to hear about Ginny's antics.

'So, we walked along the river back to my flat and....' she stopped abruptly.

Jessica came into the VIP area. She was carrying a tray filled with their drinks. She set them down on the empty table next to theirs, and placed fresh, thick papered drink mats in front of each of them. The mats were circular and black, with the Hilton's H logo occupying the centre in gold metallic.

'Thank you very much Jessica,' Josh said. He was trying hard to keep his eyes on her face, and not her none too subtle attempt to accentuate her large breasts.

Whilst Josh may have some decorum in the face of such monstrosities, Dave was looking directly at them without hesitation. Danielle was appalled, but Jessica did not appear to have even noticed. Her heavily thick lashed eyes were fixed on Josh.

'No problem at all Sir,' she said. She nibbled at her bottom lip in a clear attempt at seduction. 'I will keep an eye out and come back over when your drinks are getting low'.

'Thank you, Jessica,' Ginny said pointedly, looking at her with warning in her eyes.

'Jesus Christ,' Ginny exclaimed as Jessica retreated to the bar. 'She may as well have just served *herself* on one of these shitty little drink mats.'

Danielle laughed. It was true.

'What can I say?' Josh retorted. He flashed his winning smile at Ginny who gave him a filthy look back. She paused for a moment, then resumed her story telling.

'I need the loo,' Ginny said squirming slightly in her seat. 'I had to get to the end of that story before going, but now I'm desperate. Please hold your questions until I return. Coming?' She said, pointing her question at Danielle.

'Sure,' Danielle said, not realising until she stood that she could also do with voiding her bladder.

She had peed, wiped, flushed, washed and dried her hands, and Ginny was still peeing like a camel.

'Oh man I needed to go,' she shouted to Danielle.

Danielle was pondering whether to ask the question or not. Screw it, she thought and said, 'have you and Josh ever, you know?'

'God no,' Ginny said. She exited the cubicle, still adjusting her nude tights, 'I may have played around with a couple of men in the office, but I make it a rule not to sleep with men who a; have a girlfriend, and b; are my boss.'

'I just wondered as he seemed to know a lot about you and your escapades,' Danielle said.

'Dave, Josh and I were the last three standing at the end of the summer party. We decided to go back to the hotel bar, but when we got there, it was closed. Josh thought it would be a great idea to go to his suite and raid the mini bar. I'd never been in a posh room like that before and didn't need persuading,' she said shrugging and smiling.

'We played truth or dare, and of course, I went for truth every time, as did they more surprisingly. Naturally, the questions were about past indiscretions, so I told them about mine. Heard a lot about theirs too.'

'Interesting,' Danielle responded. She was looking at Ginny through the mirror atop the basins, 'tell me more'.

'I can't remember everything as I was on neat gin by this point, but, in a nutshell, Dave is of the opinion that, what happens once he steps over the threshold of his family home, stays outside if you get what I mean?'

Danielle turned up her nose and nodded. She knew exactly what she meant. He cheated on his wife every chance he got. Unfortunately, this came as no surprise to Danielle. Having worked alongside her fair share of businessmen, she was all too aware of what went on. Especially in the city.

These powerful men go to work, and are out of the house all day, earning stacks of cash and plying their trade. They buy sizeable homes out in the country, where they house their wives and children. The wives are usually home makers. They do not have a clue what it's like being amongst the hustle and bustle of the city. The poor businessmen feel unappreciated, and so they get their kicks fucking the young secretary, *or barmaid*! Some even spend thousands of pounds on high class escorts. They bang their frustrations away, then go home to wifey and play happy families.

The first time she had heard this sob story, she was disgusted by the pig that told her. He was playing his tiny violin, and she wanted to snatch it and shove it down his throat. 'She just doesn't understand,' he said. Classic!

But the longer Danielle spent time with these men, the more she realised that this way of living wasn't a rarity. It was almost a rite of passage. Danielle had built up an immunity to the point where she sometimes contemplated whether she has the right to call herself a feminist.

But then what could she do about it? She couldn't go and knock on Wifey's door and tell her what the cheating bastard was doing. She had however, heard a few stories of the mistresses doing just that. Becoming too dependent on these men and wanting it full time. Calling or messaging the wives to tell them all about their gross, cheating husbands.

At this point one of two things happened. The wife divorces the husband taking him for everything she can get. The mistress is then quickly disillusioned when the money dries up, and they are no longer attending Michelin star restaurants or staying in luxurious hotels. The money earmarked for these activities is now firmly in the hands of the ex-wife.

In these circumstances, Danielle imagined the scorned wife draped in diamonds and sipping champagne, counting her money and her blessings, whilst a shirtless muscled cabana boy feeds her grapes.

The second scenario when the mistress informs the wife is, wifey doesn't really care. She had lost interest in being intimate with her husband a long time ago and was happy that someone else was doing the grunt work. Mistress can continue to dine out on his dime, and suck his wrinkled dick in a five-star hotel. Wifey spends her days lunching with her friends, tending to her horses, and getting fucked by her toy boy.

Either of these scenarios generally works out better for the woman, and so Danielle could rest easy, feminist card intact.

'And Josh?' she asked, trying to sound casual and disinterested.

'He's a bit of a tortured soul,' Ginny said.

Danielle almost choked suppressing a laugh.

'Seriously. He hides it very well under layers of smarm and arrogance, but if you can get beneath the surface layers, there is a true romantic there.'

'As evidenced by his blatant flirting with our waitress. Not to mention the receptionist and secretaries in the office,' Danielle said wryly. 'All whilst he has a girlfriend back in Essex,' she finished.

'What can I say. He is young and famous. He has so many people blowing smoke up his arse, it's easy to believe the hype. And fuck me, he is gorgeous,' Ginny said, applying her lip balm, and blowing a kiss to the mirror.

'Not my type.' Danielle said this in the form of a statement. A conversation ender.

Ginny took the hint and changed the subject as they headed back out to their seats.

'Bloody hell girls, we thought you'd abandoned us,' Dave said. He had moved himself into Danielle's seat in their absence.

If she didn't know better, Danielle could easily believe that Dave also fancied a bit of Josh. The constant arse licking was just embarrassing.

Trying her hardest not to visibly cringe, Danielle moved herself next to Ginny. She glanced at her watch noting that the sun had almost set whilst they were in the loo. Eight forty-five. Still early.

'Oh god! Big boobs is hovering Josh,' Ginny said.

She thought she was being subtle nodding towards Jessica who was moving away from the bar towards them. Her pace quickened as Josh turned his head in the direction of Ginny's obvious nod.

Josh ordered more drinks and a round of tequilas. Danielle wasn't a big fan of tequila, or any shots. She had done plenty of them throughout her twenties. Back then the sole objective of alcohol consumption, was to get as drunk as possible.

These days she much preferred her alcohol to taste nice and to just take the edge off. She still liked being merry, and her inhibitions being slightly lowered. Just enough to ensure a good night's sleep, not so much that she spent half the night hugging the toilet.

Tequila appeared to have become the favoured spirit endorsed by celebrities. Off the top of her head, she could name a few. Dwayne 'the rock' Johnson, Kevin Hart, and Kendall Jenner. David Beckham had a brand too, but she wasn't one hundred percent sure whether that was tequila or gin.

'Have you had any offers to endorse tequila?' Danielle asked Josh.

'Not tequila. Vodka I have. And a few beer brands,' he said. 'Not sure it would do my reputation any good though to be honest'.

Danielle knew he was referring to the incident last summer when he got caught driving over the limit. He had smashed his car into a tree. He wasn't injured luckily, however the incident was plastered across the front page of every Sunday edition of the tabloids the following day.

The powers that be at West Ham were not at all pleased. They fined him a week's wages and, according to the papers, that cost him the mighty sum of £175,000. Thinking about that made Danielle feel sick to her stomach. It was crazy how much money is earned for kicking a ball. Some surgeons did not earn that kind of money in a year, and they saved people's lives.

Josh had the decency to hang his head when talking about the incident, and Danielle was surprised to see him display a vulnerable emotion.

The moment was short lived as Jessica big tits returned with the drinks. She had bought the bottle of 818 tequila over and handed the empty shot glasses to each of them. She took her time pouring the clear liquid into each glass, saving Josh's' glass for last. She stood back but did not retreat, waiting expectantly to observe him throw back the shot.

'Skol,' he said as he raised his glass.

'Skol,' they all mimicked his action and gulped down the shot.

Danielle shuddered as she sucked on the lime wedge that traditionally followed the shot.

'Another?' Jessica asked holding up and shaking the bottle.

'Not for me,' Danielle said, and the others followed suit shaking their heads.

'Boring,' Jessica responded looking at Danielle.

Danielle had had enough of this girl. It was one thing to hover incessantly swooping in at every opportunity like a blood starved mosquito. It was entirely another to call her boring for not wanting another shot. She was just about to tell her this when she heard Ginny.

'How about you go and shove that bottle...' Ginny started.

'Woah. Jessica, I think it would be best if you left,' Josh said, cutting Ginny off before she got herself thrown out.

Danielle was looking at Ginny, and could clearly see the internal battle she was having. She was deciding whether it would be worth it to chuck the remainder of her martini in big tits face. Josh must have been reaching the same conclusion because he stood up, placed his hand on the small of Jessica's back, and led her out of the VIP area and away from Ginny.

'That's enough for me,' Danielle said. 'I'm going to go to bed.' She knew it was time to remove herself from this situation before she lost her temper.

'Lightweight,' Dave laughed.

'Fuck off Dave,' she said, 'see you all tomorrow'.

'Bye sweetie,' Ginny said, knowing better than to try and talk her in to staying.

Danielle pushed her way through the crowded terrace, through the bar area, past the toilets and out to the elevator. She pressed the call button and was waiting for the car to arrive when she heard her name being called.

'Danielle. Are you leaving?' Josh asked.

'Yeah. I have had enough for one night,' she said.

She pointed her response to Jessica, who was standing up against the opposite wall looking flustered. She had clearly interrupted some sort of lustful embrace.

'Enjoy,' she called. The doors opened, and she stepped in to the car.

She pressed the closed-door button before Josh had a chance to answer. As the car began its descent to the seventh floor, Danielle saw the crisp white designer trainers moving away from Jessica, and towards her.

## Chapter 7

The next three days flew by in a blur as Danielle buried herself in ensuring the launch preparations were executed according to the plan. Everything was moving like clockwork. The press releases were sent out the previous day, alongside the key images of Josh modelling some of the product line. All the large news agencies, fashion journalists and influencers were invited to attend the official launch event, which would include a catwalk and a q&a with Josh.

With less than twenty-four hours to go, the whole team were busy handling their sectors. Due to the hard work and effort put into the project previously, no one was stressed, and everything was running like a well-oiled machine.

The biggest obstacle they had navigated was choosing a venue for the event. It was a time-consuming endeavour. They needed a space big enough to hold one hundred and twenty seated press, and an area to set up a catwalk. Ideally, the venue would have two separate but adjoining rooms to ensure a smooth transition, from the press conference to the walk. The location needed to be in London and easily accessible by car and train. They would also need space for a red carpet to welcome the star-studded evening guests.

Danielle made a strong case for Covent Garden. It ticked the box for accessibility, and she had found a venue that was pretty much the perfect contender.

Lucy made her case for a venue near Borough Street market. It was a short walk from London Bridge station and not far from the office. The space was light and airy, but Danielle felt it had no character. It was bland and soulless, forgettable.

The venue Danielle was batting for had *real* character. It had an auditorium that was situated under a tunnel. There was an adjoining room that was spacious enough to hold a makeshift catwalk. In particular, Danielle loved that the entire venue boasted exposed brick walls and arched ceilings. There was no natural light due to it being below ground level. She thought this was ideal for stage lighting and drawing the eye to focal points. It reminded Danielle of a bunker.

Dave had also thrown his proverbial hat in the ring with an outdoor area around green park. Danielle didn't need to voice the obvious flaw with his choice. She was secretly happy that Dave's selection was a non-starter. It meant that she was competing with just one other option.

Lucy and Danielle presented their selections to Josh for him to make the final decision. Danielle produced an audio/visual presentation. She had settled on the fact that she wasn't going to lose, so had pulled out all the stops. Danielle attempted to feign modesty. She didn't want to embarrass Lucy. Josh must have felt the same way. He acted as if he was deliberating before ultimately choosing Danielle's. She did her best to appear humble for the rest of the day. When she arrived back to her room that evening, she punched the air and did a little dance in celebration.

Now that the venue was secured, they got to work researching and hiring the external companies needed to dress the room and coordinate the event. Josh, Lucy and Danielle had spent a morning auditioning greeters. They were looking for a specific personality trait, and that couldn't be identified by looking at still images, and reading bios. Danielle found this part fun. She felt like Amanda Holden on Britain's Got Talent, sitting behind a table in judgement of the men in front of her.

She didn't attend the meeting with the model agency to audition the professionals for the catwalk. This was not her forte or part of her remit. Besides, she had plenty of other vendors to secure.

The previous day, Danielle had received an email from Josh asking her to put together some bullet points. He wanted her thoughts on the topics he would discuss in his opening speech. Josh had visited the office far more than was necessary. Almost every afternoon after training. On a few occasions, she had noticed him staring at her from his office. Danielle flatly ignored him. She thought that his request was likely an attempt to open a dialogue, but she wasn't interested in obliging.

She didn't have any real respect for him to begin with. The fact that she had caught him in an embrace with Jessica, just proved what she already thought. He was a womanising slime ball. What bothered her most was that his poor girlfriend was oblivious. She would be coming to the event tomorrow night to support him, and he had spent the last two weeks away from home. In more ways than one.

He knew Danielle would no doubt bump into Aimee, his girlfriend, at the launch. That was why he was hanging around. She was sure of it. He was trying to find the right moment, the right way to warn her off telling Aimee. The facts were it was none of Danielle's business how he managed his relationship. There was no way she was interfering.

She printed the points she had typed out, took a moment to steel herself, then walked with purpose to Josh's' empty office. She set the document on his desk, grabbed a sticky note from the wad next to his keyboard, and wrote,

*Assume this is what you were looking for?*
*Let me know if you need anything else.*
*Thanks*
*D*

Danielle stuck the note in the centre and made to leave. As she did so, she saw Josh approaching and hastened her step to get out of his office before he came in. He could see her. He quickened his own step to get to her before she could escape him.

'Danielle,' he said, attempting to block her from passing.

'I left you a note on your desk,' she said, not breaking her stride.

'Stop a minute,' his voice was low as he once again, grabbed her arm. 'I need to talk to you. Please, sit down.'

She wanted to yank her arm away and carry on walking, but knew that was unprofessional. There were still several people in the office, and she didn't want to make a scene.

Reluctantly, she sat down in the seat at the front of his desk. He followed in behind her and shut the door. He sat in his chair, pulled out a small remote from his top desk draw, and clicked a button. The glass walls frosted, shielding them entirely from the outside. Danielle had no idea his office had this capability. He had never used it before when she was around.

'I need to talk to you,' he repeated, 'and I don't want anyone else to listen.'

She looked up at his face. She didn't think she had ever seen him serious before. Today was a first. She wasn't sure what to make of it.

'I've been trying to catch your eye for days.'

'Have you? I hadn't noticed.'

'Come on. You are far too perceptive to have not noticed!'

'I've been very busy,' she said flatly.

'You know as well as I do that everything has been in place for tomorrow for weeks.' He gave her a knowing look.

'I am a professional and a perfectionist.'

'That you are. I'm happy with how everything has progressed to this point, and am looking forward to tomorrow.' His tone had softened and was less clipped. 'That's not why I want to talk to you. I want to talk about the other night.'

'With all due respect Mr Linberg, you don't owe me any explanation.' she said. She avoided eye contact, and moved to get out of her chair.

'Will you just fucking sit down for a minute and listen,' he said. 'Please,' he added realising his voice had raised.

'What you do in your spare time is your business. I know you are concerned with Aimee attending tomorrow. Please be assured, I have no intention of revealing any of your secrets.'

'I said listen.' He looked pissed off.

Danielle was again surprised to see him serious. He could be semi-serious in meetings when explaining his vision for the brand, but he always had traces of a smile. He didn't now. There was no smile evident, and he looked almost angry.

'You frustrate the hell out of me. Do you know that?'

Before Danielle had a chance to answer he continued, 'I didn't do anything with Jessica. I'm not telling you this to prevent you from telling Aimee. I'm telling you because I care what you think about me.'

Danielle was, there was no other word for it, shocked. And confused. She had never, even for a minute, thought he would be at all concerned with her perception of him. He didn't really pay any attention to her. She had spent time with him on a few occasions after work, but that was as part of a larger group.

When she first met him, it was in a Corney and Barrow dive bar next to Monument station. Lucy had arranged an introduction to make sure Josh was happy, before signing contracts. Lucy had left mid-way through lunch following a phone call from her daughter's school, so Josh and Danielle were left alone with too much food and a bottle of wine.

He was easy to talk to. She could concede that. When he didn't have the distraction of other people, he was good company. She had to admit that she had stereotyped him, so was taken aback when she realised, he was not a gormless 'man kick ball' oaf.

That meeting had been the only time they spent together completely alone. On all other occasions, he presented himself as the womanising dick that was portrayed in the tabloids.

Josh had risen to fame ten years ago when he scored the winning goal for England against Croatia in the quarter finals of the European championships. He had been subbed on in the eightieth minute as an unknown entity. The score had been a draw from the twentieth minute. It seemed nothing England tried could break the deadlock. The crowd were getting increasingly anxious and vocal. England were heading towards a penalty shootout and history had proven, they didn't end well. Josh was an unknown back then. He had been in the first team at Charlton and hadn't made any headlines.

He came on the pitch to unexcited applause. Danielle had watched this match in the pub with friends and remembered clearly. Josh was passed the ball and dribbled it past two of the opposition midfielders. He continued towards the opposition goal with two Croatian defenders fastly approaching. Head high he took aim from just outside the penalty area, and curled the ball expertly into the top right-hand corner of the goal. It was so unexpected, all the Croatian goalie could do was watch it sail past him and into the net.

Danielle remembered this well because everyone in the pub jumped from their seats cheering madly, and throwing their beers in to the air with reckless abandon. She got soaked but was so caught up in the moment, she didn't care. This memory reminded her of how young he was. At that time, she had been on a girl's holiday to Ibiza, and was legally able to drink in pubs and bars for eight years.

From that moment on, the press took a keen interest in every aspect of Josh's' life. His scoring prowess would feature on the back pages, whilst his dating exploits were often splashed across the front pages. He had moved around a few premier league clubs before settling in at West Ham three years ago.

Danielle enjoyed watching football. She had been raised in a football mad family. Her two brothers and her dad all played. When they weren't playing or discussing their own games, they were watching it on TV.

Her younger brother still played for a local club on Saturday's. Her elder brother had stopped when

Taylor was born. Now Taylor played in a little league on Sundays. The whole family were West Ham supporters and so, even before working here, she knew a fair bit about Josh.

'Why?' she said in response to his revelation. Nothing she had read and observed indicated he gave a shit about women.

He paused for a moment then said, 'because we work together. We are going to be spending a lot of time together in the next few months and I want your respect.'

'Ok,' she said.

'*Ok*?' he parroted.

'Yes, ok. I appreciate what you said. I respect your game,' she said.

She wondered if he was able to pick up on her intended double meaning of the word 'game'. He didn't say anything more. She looked at him and found that he was looking at her. From his expression he knew exactly what she meant.

A moment after the silence became awkward, he said, 'your eyes are beautiful.' There was no wink, no trace of a smile or smirk on his face.

Danielle was bemused. Was this some kind of game? It was probably a bet he had going with Dave. She could just imagine them scheming on the best way to embarrass her.

If that was the intent, she didn't fall for it. Her eyes *were* beautiful. If she did say so herself. They were also green like his, but hers were shades lighter, vivid, more of an olive green. Similarly, her skin was of an olive colouring. Danielle need only sit out in the sun for a short period of time, and her skin would darken. She supposed she must have some Mediterranean blood somewhere in the family gene pool.

Her hair was a dark brown colour. It was shoulder length, and she wore a wispy fringe at the front. Well, usually she did. Today she had worn a black headband pinning back the hair that usually hid her forehead and framed her face. She had been so busy, she had not had a chance to get it cut and hence, the headband was necessary. Without the fringe, her eyes were much more visible.

She didn't respond. She wasn't quite sure what the right words would be.

'See you tomorrow then,' she said, ending the conversation and making it clear that she was leaving the room, obstruction or not.

She needed an early night in preparation for the following day. It would be a busy one. She tapped her keycard on the door handle and paused. She had no idea how she had even got there. After leaving Josh's' office, she had no recollection of leaving the building, or travelling to the hotel. She was lost in thought. Why had he told her she had beautiful eyes? Why not just, nice eyes? Why did she have problems accepting the compliment?

'Who cares? Snap out of it!' she said to herself, crossing the threshold, and into her room.

## Chapter 8

The day was finally here, launch time. Danielle arrived at the office for six-am. She said hello to the night security guard, and took the elevator up. She was sure she would be the only one in. It was way too early for anyone else. She grabbed a coffee from the machine in the kitchen, and headed for her desk.

As she did so, the overhead lights switched on in sequence, responding to her movement. She felt like Michael Jackson in the Billie Jean music video, only in reverse. It was the ceiling lights and not lights on the floor like the video.

She plonked down on to her chair, removed her laptop from her bag, and plugged it in to the docking station. The large monitor flicked into life and the blue screen was requesting her username and password. She entered her details and got to work.

Danielle took the time to go over the day once more, so it would remain fresh in her head. They had hired the venue for three days to allow sufficient time to set up, and then dismantle the layout. The construction team would dress the room the day prior to the launch. Danielle had insisted on this to ensure they could review and refine if needed. Ginny was going to base herself at the venue for the day before and the morning of the event.

The greeters would welcome and seat the guests in the auditorium for the press conference. A mock stage would be set up with a table and chair for Josh. He would be sitting in front of a backdrop featuring the JL13 logo in multiple different colours and shapes. It mimicked the backdrop of sponsor's seen when football managers and players were interviewed post-match. The room would be lit by up-lighters in front of the backdrop, and a single light centred above the stage. The greeters would wait in the wings, ready to deliver a microphone to the journalist who wanted to pose a question to Josh.

The adjoining room would be dressed for the catwalk. A makeshift changing area would be created at the rear of the room. The catwalk would be built from large square tiles that emitted a bright white light to accentuate the design in each of the looks. A seating area would be created around the walkway spread out over three rows.

When discussing this in the meeting, Danielle's mind automatically went to a show put on by Victoria Beckham at London fashion week. The front row of her show was as eye catching as the clothing. She of course had her husband present with two out of her four children. There was a spice girl, a few NBA legends, Eva Longoria and some additional actors Danielle couldn't name. The editor of vogue magazine was also there looking the part in her huge black sunglasses. The invitees around the JL13 catwalk would be filled with journalists and influencers, so not quite as glamorous.

They had decided to hire a third room for the evening entertainment, to avoid having to mess around with set dressing. This room was on the floor above and would be dedicated to the evening guests. Danielle felt much happier about the separation as it ensured no journalists could *'accidentally'* remain at the venue for the party.

Paparazzi were invited to the outer red-carpet area to snap pictures of the arriving guests. The only media inside the venue at this point would be Josh's' vlogging team. All attendees had been advised of this prior to sending back their rsvp's.

This room also boasted exposed brick and arched ceilings. It was slightly larger than the other rooms as well as longer. Following on from the carpet, guests would be ushered inside where they would descend a flight of stairs directly into the room. The room itself would be dressed with images of Josh modelling the clothing on either side of the longer walls. Below each image would be a table, topped with goodie bags of the corresponding clothing modelled by Josh in the above image. The bags would be set out by size to make it easier for the guest to select their own freebies. Danielle felt that this was a nice touch, as it would hopefully garner additional publicity, if the attendee wore the clothes themselves.

In this room there would be spotlights above each picture. At the far end would be a DJ set up to entertain the evening guests. Danielle had negotiated with the venue to provide them with waiters and waitresses, who would hand out drinks and canapés. They were reluctant to do so at first, but conceded when she pointed out that the event would provide significant publicity for their building.

The area in front of the DJ set up would be reserved as a makeshift dance floor. Beyond this, and extending to the back of the room, they had chosen to have white circular high tables positioned in the centre. Guests would have nowhere to sit, but this was by design.

The day would begin at nine am when Josh would post the news he was launching a clothing line on his social media profiles. He was going to ask his followers to comment with any questions they had, and he would answer a selection of them live at one pm. Jarrod would then sift through the no doubt thousands of questions, and compile a list for Josh to answer. The list would be reviewed by the two of them and the press liaison, Corrin, to bullet point the dos and don'ts when he was live.

At two fifteen, the office would empty on mass into black cabs that would be waiting for them outside their building. This part was the only element that caused Danielle some concern. London traffic was notorious for its unpredictability. A journey that took ten minutes one day, could take an hour the next. She had raised this concern with Lucy but was overruled. At this stage in the proceedings, Danielle would be a mere observer. Her work was over, and the responsibility for the execution sat firmly on Lucy's shoulders.

And so, the press conference was scheduled for three thirty. Within this hour and fifteen-minute window, the press would be greeted and shown to their seats, ready for Josh to begin. They had settled on twenty minutes of Josh welcoming them and providing an overview, followed by forty-five minutes of him taking questions from the audience.

At four forty-five they would transition to the adjoining room, where they would be served drinks and seated for the catwalk. They had then built an hour into the schedule to allow for any further questions. and ensure enough time for them to depart.

The red-carpet evening would begin at seven pm, and that would conclude the team's official involvement. They were then essentially a guest too, and would be able to eat, drink and rub shoulders with the rich and famous attendees. It was at this point that Danielle had planned to take off. She would no doubt be exhausted and, schmoozing celebrities was really not her thing.

Danielle had recalled how Josh had dismissed Lucy, when she showed him the menu she had chosen for the evening canapes. She had selected small biscuits topped with crème fresh and smoked salmon, something called a caviar croute, and lobster lomain among other pretentious dishes.

He flatly refused to serve these and advised he would be serving sliders of burgers, mini pizzas, and tacos. By the look on her face, she didn't agree with that at all. Josh must've noticed as he followed up by telling her she was lucky he wasn't serving pie, mash and jellied eels. Danielle knew that would go down a treat with the native West Hammers who were in attendance. She wasn't so sure it would be attractive to anyone under the age of thirty, or anyone who lived outside of London.

She must have not been moving very much when she was firing off last minute emails, as the lights went out. They were set to turn off if there was no activity for a certain period. As she was plunged into temporary darkness, she saw a light on in Josh's' office. She waved her hands to re-trigger the light in the main office, then stood and walked over in his direction.

'Hey. I've been here for twenty minutes. I didn't see you,' she said.

'Is this another place I am not supposed to be?' Josh responded. His face in his phone and he wasn't looking up at her.

She ignored his reference to their conversation in the elevator at the Hilton and said, 'how are you feeling about the launch today? Are you nervous?'.

He looked up at her then. His brows furrowed and his forehead wrinkled as he replied, 'I don't do nervous'.

He flashed that trademark smile, but Danielle was sure there was something behind his eyes that said otherwise. Not wanting to throw him off his game on his big day, Danielle threw him an over exaggerated eye roll and earned herself a smile.

'All right then, I'll see you at nine,' she said retreating.

'Wait. Will you take a look at this for me?' he said. He was holding his phone up to her and displaying the notes app.

She took his phone as confirmation she would. He had written a few paragraphs for his press address. It was good to see that he had used some of her bullet points. She ran her eyes over his words and was, well, surprised. He had beautifully articulated what the brand meant to him, and how he was inspired by his father. She read that his parents had struggled to find affordable sportswear for him at times. His dad was a builder and his mum a homemaker. Most of their limited disposable income was spent taking Josh to and from football training, tournaments and games.

She read on learning that, at the rate he grew and the cost of boots, he would often have to wear clothes that were too short for him. Danielle was reading the last sentence when the screen changed, and a picture of his girlfriend flashed up, indicating she was calling him. She almost dropped his phone and physically jumped. She just wasn't expecting it.

'Sorry,' she said, 'it made me jump.'

She had been so lost in his words. Her imagination was conjuring up images of his mum and dad. She imagined them sat at the table in the evenings after the kids had gone to bed. They were doing calculations on an old Casio calculator, and frowning at the numbers it was returning. The image made her sad.

Danielle herself grew up as the daughter of an architect, and was afforded the luxury of getting anything she wanted as a child. She would put money on his parents being very humble despite their change in circumstances. Josh inferred that in his speech.

'It's, great,' she said. 'Really great,' she followed up. 'I wouldn't change a thing'.

She handed him back the phone as it continued to ring. His hand brushed hers as he took the device from her.

'Thanks,' he said. He was staring at his lingering fingers, before abruptly pulling away and answering the phone.

Danielle left his office, closed the door and headed straight for the bathroom. For some unknown reason, she really did not want to be in earshot of his conversation. She felt, well, she didn't know what she felt. She wondered whether it was sadness but quickly dismissed that. She couldn't stand him. That hadn't changed. But then she had read his words that were so personal and raw, and she could not reconcile them with the man she knew. She concluded that he was spinning a narrative that was sure to garner sympathy from the press, whilst simultaneously pulling at the heartstrings of his female followers. Yep, that would be it Danielle thought, even as she shook her head, knowing she was lying to herself.

## Chapter 9

The first part of the day had passed in a blur. Josh got up to one hundred thousand live views. Jarrod was flapping around worrying that he would crash the server. Danielle thought he might just crash Instagram. He spoke authentically and with passion to his fans and followers, whilst maintaining that cheeky smile and bravado throughout.

They left the office and headed down to the taxis that were waiting for them outside. Danielle felt a familiar shock jolting through her body as a hand touched her shoulder.

'You're getting in the first one with me,' he said. It wasn't a question.

She looked at her arm where his hand was, and then up at him. It was his big launch. She contemplated whether to tell him to stop fucking grabbing her, but decided she would wait until after today to do so. Her look was enough for him to take his hand away, but he was still looking at her and laughing.

They got into the first taxi. Dave went to climb in behind Josh, but Josh told him to get in the next one. The driver closed the door, got back to his seat and indicated to get back out into the traffic. Josh had sat in the seat beside Danielle, which in turn made her get up and sit on the pull-down chair behind the driver. She quickly realised this was probably worse, because she was now facing him. He still had that fucking grin on his face and her blood boiled.

'You look like you want to punch me.'

She could see he was trying and failing to suppress a laugh. He looked like a child being chastised by his mummy.

'I'm thinking about it. Launch day or not!'

'I didn't realise you had a touch phobia,' he said. He was smiling but no longer suppressing laughter.

'I don't have a touch phobia. I just don't like the way you manhandle me,' she said.

'No. I got that by the look on your face.'

'Good.'

'I wanted you to ride with me because I wanted to thank you.' When she didn't respond he continued; 'You have really shown me these past couple of months how I need to structure my business. I've always put football first and that will stay the same,

73

but seeing the way things can function here, I know I can do both. With the RIGHT staff that is,' he added.

'You have a girlfriend to factor in too.'

She looked at him. His presence filled the taxi. He really was larger than life. She had heard that there was a certain kind of presence around some celebrities. Star quality. They had something a little more than skill to make it big. It was what set them aside from the rest. Whatever it was, Josh certainly had that.

He was wearing a sweatsuit, but emanated the kind of presence she had only seen before in businessmen wearing power suits. For them, it was like they put on the suit, and it was *that* they got their power from. Like superman in his cape. For Josh, it was the man that had the presence, not the clothes. He could be wearing a bin bag, and he would still command a room. She imagined that was why he could seduce any woman. He silently demanded it. No need for words. They were putty in his hands as soon as he entered their orbit.

'Yes,' he said, raising his eyebrows. 'What I am trying to say is that I want you to stay, permanently.'

'I have my own business to run Mr Linberg,' she said. 'But I can put you in touch with some really good candidates if you're looking for another me.'

'There is no other you. That's what I'm saying. Like me on a football pitch, you just have a natural instinct. You could run this company better than Lucy.'

'Woah. I'm not stealing Lucy's job. She's a.... Friend,' she finished.

She was struggling to find the right way to describe her. Lucy was of course, not her friend. Danielle got on well with her at work. She had no interest in hanging out in her personal time.

Josh raised an eyebrow again, 'I would pay you more money. Lots more.'

'Honestly, I'm flattered but I like working for myself. I like that the only pressure I have is the kind I put on myself.'

'Take some time to think about it. I would give you autonomy.'

'Ok,' she said, if only to shut the conversation down.

He recognised that it was time to change the topic and said, 'I have two spare tickets for my box the Saturday after next. I remember you said your nephew was a big fan, I wondered whether you would like them?'

Danielle's face lit up at this. Her composure gone. She was thinking about how happy Taylor would be to go to one of the games.

'That would be amazing. He will be so excited,' she beamed as he continued.

'It's a Saturday so he won't be at school. I thought maybe you could come early, and I'll give you both a little tour. The box has full hospitality so you could eat, then watch the game.'

'Amazing. How much would you like for the tickets?'

He rolled his eyes, 'nothing. They don't cost me anything. Even if they did, I could cover it for my favourite employee.'

'I'm a contractor not an employee!' she said adding, 'don't ruin a nice moment by being a prick.'

He laughed.

'Thank you though Josh. He is going to be so stoked.'


The taxi pulled up to the kerb outside the venue. The cabbie asked Josh for his autograph, and he obliged before stepping out and holding the door open for her to exit.

She walked out to a camera flash and realised the paparazzi had arrived early. Very early. She should have expected it but was caught off guard. She was glad she had put her makeup on in the toilet before they left the office. Not that it would matter. It wasn't her they wanted the photo of.

A burley security guard was there in an instant. He stood directly in front of the guy with the camera, not saying a word. Danielle was 5 feet 7inches. She was wearing four-inch heels, yet she looked tiny next to this man. He must have been six foot six easily. He was bulky. Not fat but not muscular either. Danielle didn't blame the cameraman for taking more than one step backward.

'Cheers mate,' Josh said, and ushered her through the entrance doors and into the foyer.

The press ate up everything he had to say. They were hooked when he relayed his story that she had read earlier. The catwalk went by without a hitch. To their and Danielle's surprise, one of the men modelling the collection was Daniel Read. Daniel was also a West Ham football player. Unlike Josh, he usually shied away from the media. He must have been doing Josh a favour. It was a big one too. The photographers outside had worked themselves in to a frenzy trying to get a shot of him.

'Danielle, this is Daniel,' Josh introduced her to this vision of a man.

He was an inch smaller than Josh, which still made him a good bit taller than Danielle. His dark features made him look Spanish. His hair was cut very short, almost a buzz cut. His eyes were a chestnut brown, and were canopied by his thick, well-maintained dark eyebrows.

'Hello Danielle,' he said, taking her hand and kissing it. She watched on as his full and inviting lips lingered.

There was definitely some kind of accent there, but it was slight.

'Hello to you too,' she replied, taking in the full effect of this beautiful man.

He flashed a smile showing perfectly white teeth. Not turkey teeth white, but perhaps only a few shades darker.

It was at that moment that Aimee came over and wrapped her hands around Josh's' waist. He continued to stare at Danielle's recently kissed hand for a moment longer, before turning his attention to Aimee.

Aimee and Josh were childhood sweethearts. They met in high school and had been an item since. When Josh rose to fame, Aimee was also thrust into the limelight. They were young, normal people, suddenly exposed to money and fame. They could no longer complete a simple task, such as food shopping or fuelling their car at the petrol station.

In modern society, it was not just paparazzi that took pictures, every Tom, Dick and Harry had instant access to cameras on their phones. It was not only newspapers and magazines that served the avid gossip readers, but the internet was also saturated with blogs, vlogs and social media.

Aimee was beautiful and very photogenic. She had a model's figure and bone structure. Her flawless porcelain skin was silky, smooth and striking. She did not need to wear much makeup. Skincare brands became very interested in her routines and paid her to start endorsing their products.

Designers were captivated by her slim figure and style, and so she was offered deals to cameo on the catwalk, and to wear their clothing at public events. So much so that she was now a household name in her own right.

The shy and timid teenager had blossomed into a confident and strong-minded woman and influencer. Together, they were a power couple. They made heads turn and jaws drop.

As was typical with the journalism of the day, the tabloids dug deep to find dirt. Aimee's heartache over Josh's' infidelity was big news. Most of the media on this subject was in strong support of her, and rightly so. However, there were a few 'sources close to the couple', who were quoted advising Aimee's personality had changed. That she had less and less time for her relationship, as she spent most of her time cultivating and maintaining her public persona.

In recent years, more and more articles were written debating when they would get married and have children. Danielle had read The Metro newspaper feature that had an interview with Aimee. She sat back in her seat on the train home a few weeks ago, and learned that Aimee was sure marriage was on the cards in the near future. She explained she wanted to be married before having children and that time was running out. If that wasn't throwing down the gauntlet, Danielle didn't know what was!

'We have to get ready for the red carpet,' she told him. She took his hand and attempted to pull him away.

He stood firm and pulled her back into him. She looked up about to say something, and he kissed her long and hard on the mouth.

'Hello to you too,' he said, mimicking Danielle's words to Daniel.

Aimee took a moment to steady herself after he had completely knocked her off her feet. She looked a little dazed. Danielle thought her legs might give way. A huge grin filled her gorgeous face. She looked at him confused. It was clear that he hadn't kissed her like that for a long time.

'Let's go then,' Josh said. He took her hand and walked away without saying a word to either of them.

Danielle had watched this scene unfold in front of her with utter confusion. Not confusion about the couple themselves, confusion from the emotions she felt as a result. What was happening to her? He had somehow got under her skin. And that kiss was just downright hot. She found herself wondering what it would have been like to be on the end of that kiss.

'So, you work with Josh?' Daniel said, his sultry voice calling her back from fantasy land.

She was thankful. That was ridiculous. She must just be horny. She hadn't had sex in six months, and there were just some tensions that could not be relieved by battery operated boyfriends.

'I do indeed,' she said, turning her attention back to the stunning man standing in front of her.

Danielle had checked her watch and realised almost half an hour had passed in what only felt like seconds. Daniel was charming as well as handsome, and he had managed to make her belly laugh twice. Not an easy task!

It was almost nine-pm, and she had intended to leave at eight. The day had been such an all-consuming affair, it felt good to laugh and relax slightly.

'Are you going to introduce me to this handsome man then Dan?' Ginny asked. She handed Danielle a glass of the champagne.

'I thought if it was good enough for the rich and famous, it's good enough for us,' she said with a smile.

Danielle thought her words were ever so slightly starting to slur. She thought about telling her to slow down but caught herself. The entire team deserved to let their hair down. The event was finally over, or at least their involvement in it was, they can reward themselves.

'This is Daniel. Daniel plays football with Josh.'

'Fucking hell. Is it a requirement for all the men on your team to be drop dead gorgeous?'

Danielle choked on her drink. She coughed loudly and her eyes began to water. 'Pardon me,' she said.

Danielle was blushing, her cheeks slightly pink beneath her makeup. Ginny on the other hand, was staring at Daniel waiting for his response, completely oblivious. Daniel took a sip of his beer and set the bottle on the table.

'I'm not quite sure how to answer that question'. He put his hand out for her to shake.

When she did, he shook it and let go. Danielle found herself feeling happy that he didn't kiss it like he did hers. He was very attractive. He had a subtle self-assurance about him. Like he was comfortable in his own skin. She imagined he knew his way around a woman's body, and mind.

'I love this song.' Ginny threw her hands in the air as the DJ played a song Danielle didn't recognise.

The six-year age gap between them was never more pronounced than it was when they discussed music. In the last debate they had, Danielle found herself horrified. She had *actually* said the words, 'there's no singing in the songs these days.' She had inadvertently parroted her mum. Daphne Cooper would enter her eldest daughter's room when she was listening loudly to So Solid Crew or Oxide and Neutrino. She would walk over to the hi-fi and turn the music right down, complaining at the lack of what she called 'proper singing.'

'Do you dance Daniel?' Ginny asked. Before he could answer, Ginny had grabbed his hand and led him to the dance floor.

Danielle had her perfect chance to slip out. She didn't enjoy parties really. It wasn't her scene. She preferred to be out at a bar where the music played was in the background and you could hear yourself think. Damn it, she thought. Another one of her mother's classic lines.

The cloakroom was situated on the opposite side of the foyer. The VIP entrance was at the side of the building, so there was almost no activity at the front of the venue. Danielle was thankful for this. She didn't want anyone to see her leaving, because she knew they would try and stop her.

It wasn't because she did not have a good time, she genuinely had. She was just exhausted. If she was honest with herself, she had no desire to rub shoulders or make small talk with celebrities. It simply wasn't her scene.

Danielle collected her bag from the cloakroom. She hadn't needed to bring a jacket as the weather had been hot and dry. She exited the building and made her way to the kerb so she could hail a taxi. She held her hand out to flag down a black cab with its light on. It slowed then pulled up beside her and the driver wound down his window.

'Hilton Double Tree at Tower Bridge please,' she said.

'Yes love. Get in,' he answered

He reached up and turned off his amber light, indicating he was no longer available as she climbed in the back. The taxi was edging out into the traffic, when Danielle saw Josh running towards them.

'Sorry Sir. Could you hold on for just a moment please?' The look on Josh's face made her pretty sure he would chase the cab down if they pulled away.

'Is that....' the cabbie was squinting as Josh had reached them and pulled open the door.

'Are you ok? Why are you leaving? Was it Daniel? Has he upset you?' The words burst out of him as he panted.

'The fact you're out of breath running from there to here doesn't bode well for you,' she said, smiling.

He continued to pant.

'You need to get that fitness up son. The new season is starting.' The cabbie turned in his seat to look directly at them.

When he did, Danielle saw a West Ham air freshener hanging from the rear-view mirror. She understood now why he had stopped. It wasn't her polite request, it was because he had recognised the man running towards the car.

Danielle looked from the cabbie to Josh.

'Answer me Danielle,' he said urgently.

'Jesus. I'm fine. I just wanted to get away early as this is not really my scene.'

'So, Daniel hasn't upset you?'

'No. Why would you think that? We had a quick chat, and I slipped out when Ginny dragged him to the dance floor.'

'Ok good,' he said.

It was only at that point when he relaxed his shoulders and let out some air, Danielle realised he was so tense and wound up so tightly.

His attention turned to the cabbie, 'if I sign that air freshener for you, would you please make sure she gets back ok?'

'Absolutely,' the portly east London cabbie said.

He eagerly unhooked the air freshener and passed it to Josh. Josh scribbled his signature on it, handed it back, then closed the door and double tapped on the top of the vehicle with his hand.

What a weirdo, Danielle thought, as the taxi pulled into the traffic and headed for the hotel.

## Chapter 10

She got back to her room, undressed, and got straight into the shower. The water running over her skin was hot and powerful. It pounded her back, and she was grateful for the massage. She washed her hair and lathered her body with rich and creamy shower gel. She let the water wash all the products away, and stayed under the head for a further twenty minutes, savouring the feel of it on her skin.

When she was finished, she turned off the faucet and grabbed the large Egyptian cotton towel she had hung over the shower door. She wrapped herself tightly, then wrapped her hair with a smaller towel into a turban. She opened the bathroom door and steam bellowed out, setting off the fire alarm in the hallway.

'Fuck,' she said out loud, rushing for the chair at the vanity and pulling it towards the alarm. She stood on it and pressed the button to stop the wailing noise.

'Fuck,' she said again.

She put the chair back in its place and sashayed over to answer the room phone. Danielle spoke to a frantic receptionist with a European accent. She advised that it was the steam from her shower that set off the alarm. She eventually satisfied the woman and thought that was the end of it.

She put on her T-shirt and short pyjama combo and dried her hair in front of the vanity. She was overheating, so turned on the air con at full blast. Instantly, the colder air cooled both her and the room.

No sooner had she pulled back the sheets and got in to bed, she heard a wrap of knuckles on her door. She opened it and was disappointed to see the maintenance man standing there. She thought it may have been Josh for a moment, although why she thought that was a mystery to her.

'May I check the room please?' The badge on his overalls told her his name was Junior.

'Sure Junior,' she said, knowing that the receptionist must have asked him to check she wasn't smoking.

Inspection completed, she shut the door and pulled across the lock. She wasn't answering that door again tonight for anyone.

Danielle woke up the next morning feeling fresh and energetic. She was travelling home for the weekend. Her mum had decided to do a barbecue and had demanded all the family be there. From what Danielle could tell, she wanted everyone present before the new season started and football once again, took over the household.

Her mother had absolutely no interest in football. Daphne had ferried Danielle's father and brother's around to matches throughout their childhood. As soon as Casey, the youngest boy passed his driving test, she flatly refused to attend any more games.

She loved that her family were still close. Her mum and dad had been together for forty-five years and were still very much in love. Of their four children, Danielle was the only one who wasn't married.

Bradley was the eldest at thirty-nine. He himself had been married for fifteen years to a lovely lady called Gemma. Seven and a half years ago, after still not being able to conceive, her parents had generously paid for fertility treatment. They were pregnant with Taylor after the first try.

Taylor was the only child in the family so far, and he was spoiled rotten by all of them. Danielle couldn't wait to play him the video she hoped Josh had recorded for her, telling him about next weekend. Her brothers would be soooo jealous.

Danielle was the second of the Cooper's four children. She was thirty-five and unattached. This fact caused her mother to look at her in a pitying way that drove her nuts. Danielle had lots of boyfriends in the past. She just didn't like them enough to bring them home. She had even been engaged once. She must have known it wasn't going to end in marriage because she hadn't told her family. She took the ring off whenever she visited so they had no clue.

Next came Casey. He was a wild child. Although he was now thirty, Casey refused to let go of his twenties. He got married the previous year to a blond bombshell named Ella. Danielle didn't like Ella much at all. Though she was a saint for putting up with her brother, she was the definition of high maintenance.

They lived well beyond their means. Danielle's mum and dad had to step in not long after they got married to pay a chunk off their mortgage. They had not paid for six months, and the bank were sending some very angry letters. Their dad had seen one of those letters on their kitchen table when he went to pick Casey up for a game. Danielle was pretty sure Ella had left it there on purpose knowing that his dad would be compelled to do something about it. This was one of many instances Danielle could cite to explain her dislike for Ella.

The youngest of the Cooper brood was Ava. She was twenty-six and the quintessential baby of the family. She still lived in the family home with her new husband Derek. They were a sweet couple although, Ava could also be considered high maintenance. Ava loved Danielle dearly and was always so happy when she came home for a visit.

Danielle was spending most of her time living out of hotels however, she did have a house. It was on the road that ran parallel to her childhood home. Her dad would go round once a week to collect the post, trim the grass, and deal with any odds and sods that came up whilst she was away.

Danielle would sleep there tonight and tomorrow night, so that she could maximise her time with the family. She was proud of her home. Danielle was the only Cooper child who had not had some kind of assistance from their parents. She saved for her deposit and got herself a mortgage alone.

Of course, her father had offered to help. He had tried to insist upon it. He didn't like that she was the only one who hadn't taken his offer of assistance. It may have taken her a little longer to get on the property ladder, but she had done so off her own back.

Her business had done very well. Her income ensured she lived comfortably. She had recently been contemplating hiring more staff. The problem with that would be, that she needed to trust whoever she employed to do the job at the same standard she had built her reputation on. With a business like hers, one bad testimonial could cause irreparable damage.

She had received a number of proposals whilst she had been working with JL13. Danielle now had a backlog. It was a great problem to have but she didn't like to have to turn down business. For now, her time was taken up with JL13 entirely.

She took a cab from the hotel to London Bridge train station. It was only when she sat down on the train to Tunbridge Wells, that she took out her phone. She had two missed FaceTime calls from Ginny from the previous night, a text from Josh asking if she got home safe, and a missed call and WhatsApp message from her dad asking her to pick up some wine on her way over.

She fired off a response to her dad letting him know she would do as he asked. She then sent a message to Ginny apologising for not answering and asking how her head was this morning.

She messaged Josh, also apologising and telling him about the incident with the fire alarm.

Almost instantly he responded with, *'I heard that. Didn't know it was you.'*

Danielle was confused. That couldn't have been more than an hour or so after she had snuck out of the after party. Why was he back so early she wondered? She began typing this but stopped when her brain caught up with her. He hadn't seen Aimee for a while, he probably wanted to get some one-on-one time.

She deleted her unfinished message and put the phone back in her bag. She told herself she was too busy to care what Josh Linberg was doing. It was the weekend, and she was officially off the clock.

No sooner had she put the phone away, she felt it vibrate twice in her lap. She pulled it back out to see she had two new messages. No wait, three. Another had come through and buzzed in her hand.

The first was from Ginny, *'I feel fucking terrible. My head is killing me. I have just sent George out to get some McDonald's.'*

*Who was George?* Danielle thought as she typed back, *'I am going to need more information. At a family BBQ today. Will call this evening if you are not busy with George.'*

She received the thumbs up emoji in return, and took that to mean a call later would be fine.

The other two messages were from Josh. The first said, *'why did you stop typing?'*

The other was a video he had sent for Taylor. She had asked whether he would be able to do a quick video, but appreciated it was unlikely he would have time.

Danielle rummaged through her bag and pulled out her earbuds. She connected her phone to them and pressed play on the video.

Josh's' face and bear chest filled the screen. Danielle quickly took a look around her to make sure no one could see her screen. He had one of the most famous faces in the country. She did not want to find herself on the front page of any gossip vlogs, if another passenger saw her phone.

Satisfied no one could, she turned her attention back to the screen. The video lasted one minute and fifty-two seconds. Josh was talking to Taylor and telling him about what he would be doing next Saturday. 'Your auntie has got you the best gift,' he had said. Danielle caught herself smiling at this.

The truth was, she didn't organise any of it, Josh had. He was being so kind. He must really value her as a co-worker, she thought. She was also thinking about what it would be like to lick ice cream off of that bare chest.

She had seen shirtless pics of him multiple times. Hell, he often took his shirt off at the end of matches to swap with other players. In this video though, he had said her name, more than once. He looked directly at the camera when he did so. She couldn't deny that she was momentarily turned on. She shook her head, banishing the images of him covered in vanilla ice cream, and threw the phone back in to her bag. The video wasn't sexual, it was for Taylor!

# Chapter 11

The taxi driver drove through the gates of the Cooper property and idled on the gravel driveway.

'Nice house,' he said.

'My Dad built it,' she told him.

Everyone she ever bought home commented on the house. It made her extremely proud of her father. He was a retired architect. He commissioned the build when she, and her elder brother Bradley were young. The Cooper family moved into the property before it was entirely finished. Mrs Cooper needed to nest in preparation for the arrival of Danielle's younger brother Casey.

Danielle used her debit card to tap the card reader and paid her fayre. The driver then exited the vehicle and opened the car door for her to vacate. She did so whilst holding on to a case of wine. He opened the boot and retrieved her small travel suitcase. He set it down and pulled up the handle which he promptly handed to her.

She heard the taxi pull away as she approached the solid oak front door. She put her key into the brass lock, and entered the house, stopping in the bright atrium.

'Hello.' She called out from the high ceilinged and expansive atrium. Her voice reverberated round the room.

She waited for a response. Danielle no longer went into the belly of the house without being formerly acknowledged. The last time she did so, she found her mum and dad in a position no one should see their parents in. She still had nightmares about it.

She was glad when her mother called out to her from the kitchen, chasing away the unwelcome images her mind had conjured. Danielle made her way past the sweeping oak and wrought iron staircase in the centre of the atrium, and headed straight towards her mother's call.

She found her tending to her famous potato salad, wearing a new apron. As she turned to embrace her daughter, Danielle could see that the apron had the words; '*world's greatest Nan*' on the front.

'Love the apron mum,' Danielle said, moving forward and into her outstretched arms. 'Smells good in here,' she said to the air over her mum's head.

She was sure her mum was shrinking. Danielle could now rest her chin on the top of her head.

Daphne Cooper released her daughter from the hug but held on to her hands as she looked at her and said, 'you look lovely dear.'

'Thanks mum,' Danielle responded, knowing she could look like a sack of shit, and her mum would still tell her she was beautiful.

'Where would you like me to put these?' She lifted the case of wine she had picked up at the Marks and Spencer outside the station.

'Why did you buy six bottles?' Her mum eyed her confused.

'Ella is coming, isn't she?' Danielle smiled at her mum wryly.

'Danielle Cooper!' Her mum said by way of response, and flicked her with a tea towel. She also smiled and said, 'Put them over there for the moment. Your dad will be down in a minute.'

Danielle set them down where her mother had pointed and took a seat at the breakfast bar. Swinging her legs round she placed her elbows on the table and asked her mother how she was. Daphne launched into a story about Judy and Frank next door, and Danielle smiled as she listened.

She felt relaxed and happy for the first time in a while. Although her home was only an hour away from work, the position came with the room at the Hilton.

Danielle found herself spending more and more time at the hotel because it was closer to the office. It was also quite nice to have no household chores for a while. Her sheets were changed every day. The room was hoovered and dusted, laundry was done, and her food was prepared for her. She did miss her family though.

Geoff and Daphne Cooper liked to get the family together as often as possible. The house that was once filled with the sounds of four growing children, was now eerily quiet. Danielle looked around her childhood home, and knew she was extremely lucky to have grown up here. The house was set on a two-acre plot, surrounded by greenery and farmland. The kitchen she was sitting in was open plan and stocked with every cooking gadget or gizmo you could imagine. The breakfast bar was essentially the outer side of the kitchen island. Six tall chairs lined the bar.

Looking inward Danielle could see an eight ringed gas hob atop a double oven. The base and metal work were black. The surface space and worktops were an almost entirely black marble. Depending on which way the light hit the surface, small flecks of silver showed in the marbling. In contrast to the black oven and surfaces, the cupboards were a stark white. The handles were black and perfectly brought together the monochrome theme. The open plan kitchen was situated in the middle of the house and lit by a domed skylight. Her father had recently added some LED lighting around the base of the island, to act as an additional light source, on overcast days.

Following on from the kitchen, was a conservatory that ran the length of the house leading into the garden. The entire back wall was made up of glass panelling, each pane framed in black. The panels were pulled back against the walls either side, opening the entire room to the garden. The space itself contained a huge low back black sofa, and two white armchairs, positioned around a low oak coffee table. Dark oakwood floors ran through the entirety of the ground level.

Daphne was still chattering away when her dad entered the room.

'Hello darling,' he said.

'Hi dad,' she said planting a kiss on his cheek. 'How are you?'

'All good but I am under strict orders today so if you want to chat, you'll have to follow me.'

## Chapter 12

Danielle headed down to the lower level to help her dad with the wine. This part of the house was his domain. The whole of this floor was one large room. The theme was a spruced-up version of a dingy old English pub. To the right of the room was a bar. Mr Cooper had four different beers on draught, and it was stocked with every spirit you could possibly think of.

Deep red leather bar stools lined the outer bar aside from the very end. He had to install a lockable hatch door when Taylor started walking. Prior to the instillation, Taylor had come outside holding a bottle of Baileys Cream and shouting 'botbot'. Luckily the little tyke didn't know how to unscrew the cap.

In the centre of the room stood a pool table. There was a dartboard at the back, and a juke box separating two red leather and mahogany benches lining the left wall.

The room was lit by green glass lamps. The two tables adjoining the benches had lanterns in the centre, with melted candle wax supporting the newest candlestick. Each seat had a corresponding beer mat placed on the tables.

Shiny mahogany panelling walled the entire room. Pictures and shirts of old west ham players featured on every panel. This place was heaven to Danielle's dad. She remembered the time and care he had taken to get the authenticity just right. The room had a door that led directly to the lower garden. Outside there were two classic pub table benches. Each had a hole in the middle for parasols, that had the old school beer company branding.

Past the benches were six stone steps that led up to the main garden. A huge lawn lined with flower beds on either side, this was Daphne's domain. An apple tree stood pride of place in the centre. Modern garden furniture sat on the patio outside the main doors. The previously untouched grass expanse was now filled with all manner of apparatus for Taylor.

'Auntie Danniiiiiiii.' She heard the voice of her favourite six-year-old as he came hurtling towards her.

She picked him up and swung him round, then planted multiple kisses on his face.

'Yuck,' he said, wiping them away with his t shirt sleeve.

'Alright sis?' Bradley smiled, and leaned in for a kiss of his own. 'Where's dad?'

'In the bar,' she answered. She put Taylor down, and he went running ahead of Bradley eager to get to his grandad.

Before long everyone had arrived. As was typical at these events, the men were sitting outside the bar whilst the women were on the lawn terrace. Taylor was having a whale of a time running from swing to slide to paddling pool.

Danielle had got confirmation from her brother and sister-in-law that she could have Taylor for the day next Saturday. She called everyone to the bar tv.

'I've got a surprise for you Taylor Cooper,' she said beaming at him.

'Show me,' he said

She picked him up, put him on her lap, and pressed play on the video she had synced up to the tv. Taylor screamed with excitement as soon as he saw Josh's' face on the screen.

106

'Jesus,' Ella said looking at the screen like she wanted to climb inside. Danielle shot her a look that told her to be quiet so Taylor could hear.

When Josh had finished talking, Danielle disconnected her phone and said, 'what do you think about that?'

'Wow mate, I'm jealous,' Bradley said to his son.

'Me too,' said Casey

'And me,' said her dad

'And me,' said Ella, earning herself an evil from Casey.

'How many sleeps is it?' Taylor asked Danielle.

'Seven,' she answered.

'I can't wait to tell everyone at school.'

'Sis. Can you send me that video? I wanna show my boss. He will die!' Bradley asked.

'Sure,' she said and forwarded the video.

Danielle spent the next hour fielding questions about Josh and the launch.

'Can you bring him over next time we have a barbecue?' her dad asked. Deadly serious.

'Erm no. He's my boss, not my friend.'

'You looked pretty friendly in the picture I saw on my feed this morning,' Ella said. She was attempting and failing to hide her jealousy.

'What picture?' Danielle asked confused.

'This one,' Ella said showing it to them all on her phone.

It was the picture the pap took of them when they had gotten out of the taxi. Danielle had not realised he had managed to get another shot of them. This one featured Josh, his hand on her lower back guiding her through the entrance.

'Please tell me I'm gonna get a West Ham legend as a brother-in-law.' Casey had almost lost his mind.

'No for fucks sake.'

'Danielle. Language,' her mum chastised.

She looked around and spotted Taylor with his headphones on, watching something on his iPad inside, 'he can't hear me'.

Josh had been the topic of conversation for almost the entirety of the day. After she'd had her food, Danielle was ready to leave.

'It's only seven, and I thought you were going to stay here tonight?' her mum said when she announced she was leaving.

'I have stuff to do at the house. I'll see you tomorrow.'

She hugged and kissed everyone goodbye and exited out of the side gate, eager to duck out of the interrogation.

# Chapter 13

She made the short walk to her house and almost ran down the path and inside. She closed the door behind her and let out an audible sigh of relief. She loved her family dearly, but this Josh thing was annoying. She knew they would have questions but Jesus!

Her home was a modest three-bedroom semi. When she bought it six years ago, she had done so knowing it would be a work in progress. The previous owner was an old lady who hadn't updated the decor since the early eighties.

Danielle had systematically decorated room by room. She had spent her weekends looking at colour pallets and carpet samples. She had done most of the painting herself. Casey had a friend who was a floor layer. He had done the carpet and wooden floors throughout the house.

Her favourite part of the renovation was dressing the rooms once they had been transformed. She spent hours scouring the internet to find furniture that complemented each room perfectly.

She enlisted the assistance of her dad to build an en-suite for her master bedroom. It was a lot more hassle than she had initially anticipated. Upon reflection, the hard work was certainly worth it. Her walk-in shower and rolled top bath were two of her favourite investments.

The only part of the house that she didn't have an interest in doing herself, was the garden. Danielle hated gardening. She let her mum loose on the front and back outside areas. She gave her a budget and just let her do whatever she wanted. Her only stipulation was that it be low maintenance. She would not be pruning flowers or preening bushes.

She finished doing the bits she needed to get done and sprawled herself out on the sofa. She switched the tv on and fell into a deep sleep. Vibrating woke her up with a jolt. It took her a minute to work out where she was. She scrambled for her phone and saw Ginny was Face Timing.

'Hey!' she answered yawning.

'Please don't tell me I woke you up? It's 10pm on a Saturday.'

'I was fast asleep. I have had a long arse day.'

'Wanna talk about it?' Ginny asked.

'No,' she said flatly. 'I'm ready to hear about yesterday.'

'Oh. My. God,' she started, then launched into a story that Danielle wouldn't have believed if it were anyone other than Ginny telling it.

Apparently, Aimee had gotten very mad when Josh had run out of his own launch night to come after Danielle. Aimee had gotten herself blind drunk and started a row with Josh in the middle of the foyer.

Ginny had overheard this exchange when she was coming out of the ladies. She hid behind a large pillar so she could hear more about what was going on.

'Josh was trying to calm her down and appease her explaining he was just checking you were ok,' Ginny told her. 'They were heading back inside when I heard her say, 'stay away from that fat bitch.'

Danielle's throat went dry. She sat up and felt the overwhelming urge to be sick, 'she said what?' Danielle managed to get out.

'Well. Get this. Josh stopped dead when she said it. He pulled his hand out of hers and he said something to her in a low voice that I couldn't hear.' Ginny paused for dramatic effect. 'Then he turned and walked out. On his own event. Just left her there stunned.'

'We messaged this morning, and I thought it was weird he said he heard the fire alarm I set off. I just thought he'd left early for some alone time with her!'

'What fire alarm?'

Danielle briefly explained and when she had finished, she just stared at Ginny at a loss for any more words.

'Oh, and Daniel was asking me lots of questions about you.'

'Was he?' If she had heard this news first, she may have been excited. Hearing it after the earlier news, made it pale in comparison.

'Yeah girl. You got these men eating out of your hand.'

'I don't think so. Listen. I'm glad you're feeling better, and I want to know all the details about the man that was in your bed this morning, but I'm exhausted. Can we get lunch on Monday?'

'Sure,' Ginny said, looking concerned.

'Great. See you Monday,' Danielle said and ended the call.

What the fuck is going on? She thought to herself.

Well, Aimee was clearly awful about her, but she was upset seeing her boyfriend chase after another woman. It wasn't like that. He was just checking she was ok. He didn't get in the taxi, he stood outside it. He did run though.

Heat, exhaustion and Pinot Grigio combined with that phone call, made Danielle run to the downstairs bathroom and throw up. She didn't want to be the cause of any drama. She hadn't done anything wrong.

Aimee's insecurities are not her problem, Danielle settled. In any case, she was the one in a relationship with someone whose infidelities were splashed all over newspapers. Clearly, she had accepted that BS, so why draw the line with her? And to call Danielle a fat bitch was just cruel.

## Chapter 14

Danielle spent the whole of Sunday at home. She had text her mum to tell her she wasn't feeling well and didn't want to leave the house. She lounged about in her sweats watching crappy tv, ordering pizza and eating ice cream.

At seven pm she decided she was going to get a taxi all the way to the hotel. She couldn't face the train. She would put the cost of it on her expenses and if she was queried, she'd tell them exactly why.

She scurried through the foyer and headed to the elevator, eyes pointed at the floor. She didn't want to make eye contact with anyone. She made it to her room unhindered and took a look at herself in the bathroom mirror.

'Pull yourself together Cooper,' she said to her reflection.

Fifteen minutes after she had arrived in her room, there was a knock at the door. She looked through the peephole and felt the knot form in her stomach when she saw Josh standing there. She didn't answer.

'I know you are in there,' he said through the door.

She didn't answer.

'I'm not leaving until you open the door.'

He knocked continuously for what felt like an eternity and made Danielle want to punch him in the face.

'Stop!' she said. That was it. One word. Clearly, he had asked the front desk to let him know when she got back. His insistence told her as much.

'When someone knocks on your door, you are supposed to answer it'.

'I don't want to talk to you today,' she said by way of a response.

'Tough.'

Who did he think he was? She would barely tolerate this bullish attitude at work, she certainly wasn't going to have it in her own time.

'I'm not answering the door so just fuck off.'

She heard him grunt in frustration.

'Just open the fucking door,' he shouted and pounded the door in irritation.

As he did so, Danielle yanked the door open, and he almost fell into her. She stepped back and he steadied himself. In one swift movement he lunged forward and grabbed her arms. This was becoming his signature move. Before she knew what was happening, they were nose to nose, eyes locked. She stood rooted to the spot for a moment, then pulled away and yanked her arms free.

'What the fuck are you doing?' she said, furious.

'I need to talk to you. I need you to hear from me before you're told by someone else.'

'That your girlfriend called me a fat bitch? Too late I already heard.'

She sat on the bed with her back against the headboard and drew up her knees, hugging herself. He sighed and fell into one of the chairs next to the coffee table.

He ran his fingers through his hair and blew out his cheeks. He didn't speak for a moment and Danielle was sure he was trying to work out what to say. He went with, 'she didn't mean it.'

Danielle scoffed. 'Fuck off Josh. She meant it.'

'She didn't. She was drunk and annoyed that I ran outside to you. She got jealous.'

'Jealous?' Danielle said incredulously. 'What the fuck is there to be jealous of? We work together. That's the end of the story.'

'She was just drunk,' he said again.

'If that's the case, do you want to tell me what you said to her before you walked out?'

'That's not any of your concern,' he said, trying not to show surprise at how much she knew.

'The fuck it isn't! You have come to my door and pounded on it for twenty minutes, and when I finally answer, you don't want to say?'

'For fucks sake Danielle. You're driving me crazy!'

'Me? What am I doing? I'm doing nothing. It's big tits Jessica she should be mad about'.

As soon as the words came out, she knew she had gone too far. He looked mad. She stared him down. She was fed up with feeling like a victim. She was determined not to break the stare. To her surprise, he did and as he did, he got up and left.

Danielle watched him leave without saying anything. When she heard the door click shut, she shut her eyes and cried.

## Chapter 15

Josh didn't come to the office the next day. Or the next. Or the next. By Friday, Danielle was wondering whether the invitation for Saturday's game had been withdrawn. She hoped not. Not for her, but for Taylor. He was so excited. Bradley had been sending her little videos of him singing 'I'm forever blowing bubbles'.

When she returned from lunch out with Ginny, Danielle found an envelope on her desk. It was a plain manilla envelope with nothing written on the front. She picked it up, opened it and saw two lanyard passes to go around their necks for entry to the stadium. She poured them out on the desk to take a closer look. On top of the two passes was a piece of a4 paper folded in half. She picked it up and read,

*'I will send a driver to pick you up at 9. If Taylor can't stay with you tonight, we will get him in the morning.'*

That was it. More demands and commands. This man really made her mad. He also sometimes made her feel lightheaded and giddy. She was so angry with herself for allowing her brain to entertain him. It was a pointless and futile exercise really. He was fucking with her head.

Danielle reminded herself that this was for Taylor, took a deep breath and pulled out her phone.

'Hey Bradders,' she said when her brother answered.

'Everything ok?' He sounded panicked.

'Yes, all good.'

'You never call me.'

'I'm just calling to ask whether Taylor could stay with me tonight? Josh has sorted a driver to pick us up and take us to the stadium,' she asked.

'Sure. I'll bring him to you after work. Will you be back there by six?'

'I'll make sure I am. We can order room service and watch a movie.'

'Make sure he is asleep by eight-thirty, or you'll know about it tomorrow.'

'Yes yes,' she said. 'Love you, bye.'

Danielle went down to reception to collect Taylor. She sat in the lounge opposite the reception desk and hoped wholeheartedly not to see Josh come in. She heard Taylor before she saw him. He was running and his shoes were squeaking as he shouted her name.

'Shhhh,' Bradley told him, but Taylor was too excited to even register his dad's command.

'Hello beautiful,' Danielle said as he jumped into her lap.

'Thanks Dan. I don't think we would have got any sleep if he stayed at home tonight. Here is his bag.' He handed the bag to Danielle who stood up and took it.

'Right then,' she said taking Taylor's hand, 'say bye to daddy.'

'By daddy.'

'Bye baby,' Bradley said through mock sadness. 'Clearly doesn't care about me right now.'

'We'll facetime tomorrow,' she said.

Bradley made his way back to the doors he entered through less than two minutes before.

Danielle let Taylor press the keycard to call the lift. It took him a few tries, but he managed it. They headed up to the room and perused the menu for their dinner.

Taylor selected a pizza whilst Danielle ordered a chicken salad. She had a big lunch and wasn't too hungry. She opted for no dessert, but Taylor asked for chocolate ice cream. Once they had called down to the kitchen to give their order, they turned their attention to the movie listings. Taylor chose the new power rangers movie. She would just play on her phone whilst he watched.

The food arrived promptly and they both tucked in. Danielle was amazed when he had finished his plate.

'You are getting so big,' she said to him. 'I can't believe you ate it all.'

'I need to be big and strong,' he said, showing her his *'guns'*.

'Wow!' she said, trying not to laugh at his little face.

She put the plates on a tray and set it down just outside her door to be collected. Danielle was about to press play on the movie when her phone rang. She looked at it and saw Josh was trying to Facetime. Her first instinct was to cut off the call, but she couldn't do that to Taylor. Danielle wondered whether Josh new that when he decided to call.

'Hello,' she answered, looking at the screen and the face that filled it.

'Have you got him?' he asked. To the point as always.

'Yes, I have him and hello to you too,' she said. 'Hold on a sec.'

She looked into the eyes of the little boy sitting next to her. He was a bit confused, and she could see little frown lines appearing on his forehead.

'I have someone here that wants to speak to you. Is that ok?' she asked him.

He nodded his ascent still looking weary. She passed him the phone and his face was a picture. Danielle wished she had her own phone to capture this moment.

'Hello mate,' Josh said to Taylor. 'I'm looking forward to seeing you tomorrow. Are we going to win do you think?'

Taylor didn't answer at first and she thought maybe he was going to be too shy. A beat later he said, 'yeah of course we are going to win, and you are going to score.'

Josh laughed and Danielle's stomach flipped. He sounded so carefree as he chatted away with Taylor. There was no hint of the man that had stood in this very room less than a week earlier. She felt vulnerable and the emotion was not welcome. She was not going to get sucked in to this head fuck.

Taylor wanted to FaceTime his dad and grandad to tell them about Josh's call. Danielle took the phone from Taylor, fired a quick thank you text to Josh, and made the group call. She also included Casey. He would want to be involved.

She passed the phone back to Taylor and went to the bathroom to run him a bath. She could hear Taylor excitedly relaying details of the call with Josh and smiled. At least he wasn't taking their argument out on this little boy.

She poured a generous amount of bubble bath in the tub and left the water running. She went back out into the main area of the suite, and stood behind Taylor waving at her dad and brothers.

'We need to go now buddy,' she said to Taylor. 'Your bath is ready.' She took the phone back and said goodbye, ending the call.

Taylor was bathed, pj's were on, and he was tucked up in bed next to Danielle. She put the movie on knowing that he would not get to the end of it. His eyes were heavy. He was struggling to keep them open.

As she suspected, he was out of it by eight thirty. Danielle sent a quick text to Bradley advising him of her abeyance to the rules, snapping pictures of a sleeping Taylor as evidence.

She used the remote to change the channel. Usually, she would watch some kind of murder documentary. She decided against it just in case Taylor woke up. She settled on Friends reruns.

## Chapter 16

'Wake up auntie Dan'. Taylor was shaking her and bouncing on the bed. She groaned and looked at the clock.

'Shit. I mean poo,' Danielle said, not believing the alarm clock that told her it was eight am. She looked over at Taylor who was already dressed and laughing.

'You said a bad word,' he told her.

'Sorry buddy. Wow! You are all dressed and ready to go,' she added, changing the subject. 'There are coco pops and a bowl over there and milk is in the fridge,' she said pointing to the areas he could find the items. 'Do you think you could make yourself some breakfast whilst I get ready?'

He nodded.

She decided to go with a black full trousered jump suit. It was muted and non-descript but flattering. The lightweight material caressing her curves in an understated fashion. Danielle accessorised with a thin cream belt pulling her in at the waist, cream open toed wedges, and a pair of gold hoop earrings. She went light with the makeup opting for tinted moisturiser over foundation, black mascara and a red lip gloss. The gloss highlighted and darkened her lips slightly. The look was overall, natural.

She plaited her hair, not wanting it in her face in case she got too hot. She applied suncream to her arms and chest then covered Taylor in factor 30. She popped the bottle into her Ted Baker shoulder bag, knowing she would need to top him up at some point during the day. She rummaged through the vanity draw and found her Ted baker sunglasses and shoved them on the top of her head. She took her Jean jacket off the hanger in the wardrobe and draped it over her arm. She was too hot to wear it right now.

'Have you cleaned your teeth?'

'Yes,' he said avoiding her eye.

'Don't tell fibs. Go and do it now and we will head down.'

Danielle took one last look at herself in the full-length mirror. Her freshly cut wispy fringe was not playing ball, but she didn't have time to deal with it, so it would just have to do.

'Ready,' Taylor said, wiping his mouth on the towel and showing her his cleaned teeth.

'Miss Cooper.' The driver tipped his hat and opened the rear door to invite her and Taylor inside.

'Thank you,' she said.

She ducked down to follow Taylor into the large and sleek estate car. She buckled Taylor in, then affixed her own seatbelt. The driver had returned to his seat at the front but had not yet pulled away. He picked up a claret and blue gift bag that was sitting on the passenger seat.

Handing it to Taylor he said, 'Mr Linberg got a little something for you.'

Taylor opened the bag and pulled out the brand-new kit for the season complete with Cooper and the number 13 on the back. He squealed with delight.

'Can I wear it today?' he asked Danielle.

'Of course you can. We can put your old one in the bag to take home.'

He threw his old shirt at her and eagerly put on the new one. She opened the bag to put the old shirt in and noticed at the bottom, a large bag of sweets

129

and a cylindrical container. She pulled out the container and realised it was bubbles.

'Look what else you have got,' she said, showing Taylor the sweets and bubbles.

'I'm so lucky!' he exclaimed, and Danielle's heart melted.

'You will have to thank Josh when we see him won't you?'

Once they were approaching the stadium, Danielle retrieved the lanyards from her bag. She put one round her own neck and the other on Taylor. She took out her phone and snapped a picture of him in his new shirt.

'Cheeeeeeese,' he was holding his pass up at the camera.

She sent the pic to her family group chat. Her brothers would be dying! The car pulled up outside the players entrance and she dropped her phone back in her bag.

The driver held open the door for them both to exit.

They were met at the stadium entrance by a young man named Craig. He introduced himself as an usher. He glanced at their passes subtly checking their authenticity. He outlined the schedule for the morning, then led Danielle and Taylor up some escalators and across a long hallway, to the Linberg hospitality suite.

'Mr Linberg will be with you shortly,' he said, 'Please make yourselves at home. Is there anything I can get for you whilst you wait?'

She shook her head and said, 'thank you very much Craig.'

Danielle walked in the room and was instantly struck by the large image of Josh taking up the whole wall on the left. He was on the pitch in full kit, hands up in the air in celebration. His smile was one of absolute elation. It made Danielle smile looking at it. His hair was slicked back and wet with sweat and rain. His shorts and socks were stained with green and white, indicating he must have been tackled to the floor more than once. The small part of his thighs on show between his shorts and socks was tight. Every muscle was engaged. Danielle thought she could see the outline of his cock through his shorts and blushed a little.

Of course, it would be that moment Josh came through the door. Luckily, she had put her sunglasses on to shield her eyes from the bright rays coming through the all glass wall, that led out to the stands. Taylor had already opened the door and was standing out in the open-air seating taking in the ground. He looked so tiny in the humongous stadium.

'Morning,' Josh said as he walked forward and planted a kiss on her cheek. 'Your face is warm,' he stated.

'Yes, well, it's a warm day,' she responded cringing inwardly. If only he knew why her cheeks were *actually* hot and red.

He passed by her and headed out of the door to the stand where Taylor was.

'Alright buddy,' he said, and held out a hand for him to shake.

Taylor ignored this and flung his arms round Josh embracing him and thanking him for his new shirt. Danielle's knees almost gave out as Josh hugged him back and picked him up bringing him back inside.

'Look,' Josh said to Taylor. 'We have actually managed to make auntie Danielle genuinely smile.'

She poked her tongue out at them in response and they all laughed.

Taylor took Danielle's hand as Josh led them around on a tour of the stadium. They started by being shown around the team's gym. A few people were working out. Danielle didn't recognise them so assumed they were not part of the first team. Josh sat Taylor on one of the rowing machines, strapped him in and showed him how to use it. She took a seat on one of the weightlifting apparatus and watched them get on with it.

From the gym, they made their way to the players restaurant. It was much busier in there and Danielle found herself feeling a bit out of place. There was something uncomfortable about intruding on people who were eating. Like watching animals through glass at the zoo.

They didn't seem phased. They were probably used to this type of intrusion. Josh introduced them to some of the players and coaches. Danielle recognised a few from the launch party. Taylor's little hand gripped Josh's tightly and refused to let go. This was such a big moment for him. He was looking around in pure wonderment.

Josh found an empty table and they sat down whilst he went to order drinks. Danielle went with water as it was too hot for coffee, and too early for alcohol. Josh had the same and Taylor chose apple juice. He returned to the table with the drinks and one additional item. He handed Taylor a big wedge of chocolate cake. Taylor's eyes lit up like it was Christmas morning. Danielle thought *this* year's Christmas morning would pale in comparison to this day. She smiled, inwardly thinking about how she had one up on her brother.

'What do you say?' Danielle asked.

'Thank you Josh,' Taylor replied, eyes wide as he contemplated where to start.

By the time Taylor finished eating, he had chocolate all round his mouth, and in his teeth. Josh found it hilarious and took his own phone out to take a picture. Danielle thought this was really cute. It was nice observing him with her nephew. He was genuinely interested in making sure Taylor had a good time.

After Danielle had cleaned the chocolate from his face and hands, they made their way to the trophy and memorabilia room. The last time West Ham had won a league was in 1981. they had never won a premier league title. It was at this point Danielle asked Josh if she could face time her brothers. He said it was fine and so she made the group call, and handed the phone to Taylor. Taylor was giddy with delight, and pretty hyper after the gigantic piece of chocolate cake he had just demolished.

Casey joined the call first and Taylor launched into a rundown of the day so far. He repeated it again when Bradley, accompanied by their dad and Derek joined.

'Show them where you are now then,' Danielle urged him.

He was having trouble getting the right angle to show the trophies and so, to Danielle's disbelief, Josh took the phone and filmed Taylor for them. She was surprised when Taylor sat on Josh's' knee, and he turned the camera to face them both. Casey almost lost it.

'Oh my god,' he shouted, 'nice to meet you mate.'

Casey had the biggest, most stupid grin on his face. His outburst caught the attention of Ella, who upon realising what he was shouting about, stood behind him and waved.

'Hi all. We are just showing young Taylor here around the stadium,' Josh told them.

'We are going to go on the pitch soon,' Taylor said excitedly.

'That's so good mate,' Bradley said beaming. 'Make sure auntie Dan takes lots of pictures.'

'She is. Me and Josh made her smile earlier didn't we Josh?' Taylor was giggling.

'We did. It was nice to see, wasn't it? She doesn't smile very much at work.'

Danielle exaggeratedly rolled her eyes and said, 'I smile loads at home. You just don't give me much to smile about.'

There. Have that, she thought. Josh laughed, and Danielle took advantage of Taylor's attention being elsewhere to flip him the bird. That only served to make him laugh harder.

Completely out of character, Ella was asking Taylor questions. At one point she had spoken over their dad, drowning him out with her over exaggerated girly voice. She was so transparent. Usually, she paid next to no attention to Taylor. Danielle, once again rolled her eyes. She started asking another question when Josh interrupted her.

'Sorry, we have to get going. We're on a schedule,' he said.

Danielle could only imagine how Ella reacted to that. She wasn't used to men not giving her their undivided attention. She would be embarrassed. Good. Danielle thought.

Josh ended the call and let out a long whistle, signifying he knew exactly what Ella was trying to do.

'She always like that?' he asked Danielle.

'Well, she certainly isn't usually so interested in Taylor's life. That's for sure.'

'Not a fan?' He said.

'What makes you say that?' she said, making sure the answer was obvious to him, but not to Taylor.

'Let's go see the dressing room.'

In the home team's dressing room, all the players shirts were neatly hung above each person's assigned seat. She noticed Josh's' seat was next to

Read's. Behind where the shirts were hung, each player had a locker for them to store the rest of their kit and the clothes they arrived in.

Danielle took pictures of Taylor in front of all his favourite player's shirts. Josh picked up a ball from the middle of the room that was sitting on top of a laundry bag full of towels, and started doing kick ups. Taylor counted loudly for each one.

'Want to go on the pitch?' Josh asked.

'Yes, please.' Taylor was already running towards the door.

They walked out of the dressing room, and into the tunnel Danielle always saw the players lining up in on the telly. It was surreal seeing it in front of her. As she walked, her wedges made a clapping count with each step that echoed. She could almost hear the clacking noise of the men's studs as they walked out to the pitch.

Josh and Taylor ran ahead and out on towards the goal. Danielle opted to stay off the grass and sat in the stands behind the manager's seat. It didn't feel right to sit there for some reason.

Josh played goalie as Taylor took little run ups and kicked the ball in the net. Danielle had to zoom in, but she managed to film it. She was smiling away and then, through the zoom, she could see Josh looking for her. He spotted her after a moment, and sent her one of his trademark smiles. Once again, she felt the increasingly familiar, and completely unwelcome pang deep in her stomach. She flatly refused to acknowledge or accept what that meant, and pointed the focus on Taylor.

If she believed, she would have sworn it was divine intervention that bought her back to the present. Daniel Read slid into the seat next to her and planted a soft kiss on her cheek. Panic rose up in her and she checked to see if Josh had seen this.

She relaxed a little, as he continued playing with Taylor, seemingly oblivious.

'Hello beautiful,' he said brazenly. 'I was sad to see you had left the other night without even saying goodbye.'

'Sorry about that,' she responded. 'I was very tired and needed to go home. Besides, it looked like Ginny had entertaining you covered.'

'Is that what you were doing? Entertaining me?' He placed a hand ever so gently on her thigh.

She looked at his mesmerising eyes and said, 'If anything, I stayed longer than intended because you were entertaining me.'

She broke away from his gaze, she had to. He was looking at her like he wanted nothing more than to entertain her. In every possible way. He took come to bed eyes to a different level.

He started to say something, but stopped abruptly as a football came sailing over their heads and landed in a seat directly behind them.

'Oops!' Josh said as Taylor laughed, 'sorry.'

He said the words but they both knew he meant for that ball to land exactly where it did. The two men locked eyes. Danielle looked from one to the other feeling uneasy. Luckily, Taylor was completely unaware of the blatant display of male testosterone being showcased right in front of them.

It was at that moment that a few of the other players had come out on to the pitch to start warming up. Danielle was thankful.

'I better get changed and out on the pitch to warm up,' Daniel said.

He stood up, took her hand, and placed another kiss on it. Daniel took the long way back inside to avoid getting too close to Josh. Danielle didn't blame him. Josh looked like he wanted to kill someone. Like he wanted to kill her.

Danielle didn't know how she had ended up in a fucked-up relationship, whereby Josh was allowed to stop her from talking to other men, whilst he was shacked up with a blonde bombshell. A bombshell that recently said awful things about her.

Well fuck that. Danielle was single and could do whatever the fuck she liked. She stood up, took Taylor's hand, and ushered him inside, back to the hospitality suite.

Josh had the wherewithal not to follow her. If he did, she may well have caused damage that rendered him unable to play football that day. Fucking hell, he infuriated her. Now wasn't the time to dwell on it though. Today was about Taylor and she would be damned if she'd let it be ruined.

# Chapter 17

It was half an hour before kick-off. Danielle and Taylor had just finished eating a delectable cheeseburger and chip lunch. It was delicious. Once again, Danielle hadn't realised she was hungry until the food was placed in front of her, and her stomach growled at the smell of it.

Craig came in to clear the table, and was followed by a man she instantly recognised as Josh's' dad. He smiled at her, and Danielle had to do a double take. The smile was so familiar, he looked like Josh. Or Josh looked like him more accurately.

Dale Linberg was an older gentleman. Danielle would put him in his sixties. His age didn't detract from his looks. He was handsome. He had grey hair and a neatly manicured beard. A slightly large belly could be seen through his dress shirt, but it wasn't overhanging.

'You must be Danielle,' he said. He sounded just like Josh. His eyes sparkled like Josh's' did. It was surreal.

'And this,' he said, walking over to shake Taylor's little hand, 'must be Master Cooper. I see you are wearing the new shirt my son got for you!'

Taylor went a bit coy, not unlike most six-year-olds did when meeting strangers.

'Hello Mr Linberg,' Danielle stood to shake his hand. 'Taylor, this is Josh's' Daddy.'

They stood and spoke for a few moments and Dale had told her his sister and brother-in-law would also be joining them in the box. Danielle remarked on the similarity between he and his son. She was certain he had heard that a thousand times before. She found herself at ease speaking with his family, and was grateful they made the effort to include her and Taylor.

'My wife and daughter were supposed to come with us,' he said. 'Unfortunately, they have both caught a bug.'

'There does seem to be something going around at the moment. I hope they recover quickly,' she said. 'If you don't mind, Taylor is eager to get outside to watch the team warm up?'

'Of course, we will be out there shortly.'

Danielle opened the door that led out to their seats in the stadium, and was hit with an overwhelming and unmistakable sound. She had been to many games over the years, and the atmosphere at a home ground on match day could not be replicated anywhere else. It was sensory overload, and she wondered whether it was a bit much for Taylor. She looked at him to check but he seemed completely unphased.

Danielle wondered if that was why Josh had given him a tour and taken him out on to the pitch, to help him feel more comfortable in this environment. She would thank him for that later. She hoped that by then, enough time would have passed for both of them to have calmed down.

They sat down in their seats and looked down on to the pitch. They were quite a way up. In fact, Danielle was quite sure they were at the very back of the stands. Each of the ten seats in their area had iPads assigned to them, so they could see the game closer if they wanted to. They were also sat just along from the large monitor in the stadium.

Danielle's heart fluttered a little when she looked at the big screen and saw that the cameraman was focusing on Josh. He had a fluorescent orange bib over the top of his training kit, and was warming up by running on the spot. The camera zoomed in on his face and he still looked mad, making her feel a pang of guilt. She really hoped that she was not the cause of his anger. She didn't want to be the reason for him being off his game on the pitch. She'd never go to a game again if that was the case.

Before long, the large screen was showing both teams as they lined up in the tunnel waiting for their cue to come out. The commentators were talking over the images of the players at the front of the line, giving their score predictions, and discussing possible tactics. Danielle found herself looking for Josh. She spotted him towards the back and her heart leapt into her mouth.

She couldn't make out entirely, but could see him talking to Daniel and was sure she lip read Josh saying, *'fucking stay away from her.'*

She listened closely to see if the commentators had picked up on the tension but thankfully, they remained oblivious.

The line began moving out on to the pitch and the crowd roared. Taylor was blowing his bubbles and shouting. Danielle jumped as she heard Dale whisper to her. He was being as quiet as possible, but loud enough so she could hear above the crowd, 'are you the 'her' he was talking about?'

She froze. She didn't know what to say. She was absolutely the *'her'* Josh was talking about but didn't want his dad to kick her out.

'Can you come inside with me for one moment?' he asked her. 'Taylor will be fine.'

She told Taylor she would be back in a minute and followed Dale inside. When she entered, he shut the door behind them.

'Give us a minute Craig please.' It wasn't a question.

So familiar, Danielle thought. She looked at him trying to keep her face neutral and impassive.

'Look Danielle,' he started, his tone shooting right through her. 'My son has spoken very highly of you. Too highly in front of his fiancée.'

Danielle's legs gave way, and she fell into the seat just inside the door. Fiancée? Since when?

Looking at her face, he paused a moment, then Dale carried on; 'Aimee and Josh have been together a long time. I know he had been a bit of a boy in the past, but he is changing all that. I know better than most that there comes a point where you have to stop fucking about and settle down, and that's what he's doing,' he carried on. 'Now I'm

146

not telling you to stay away. I don't presume to know what is going on between you. All I'm saying is, I don't want him to undo all the hard work he has done over the last year.'

Danielle just stared at him. Her eyes stinging as she tried to hold back angry tears. He sat next to her and put a caring hand on her shoulder.

'I didn't mean to upset you love. Secretly, I'm rooting for you. I've never seen a sparkle in his eye like he gets when he talks about you. His mum and sister on the other hand, are very close to Aimee.'

It was at this point that Danielle decided she wasn't going to be cast as the femme fatale in this fucked up little scenario. She told his dad everything. From the roof top bar, to the launch night with Daniel, to the bursting through the door of her room in the hotel.

He sat back and exhaled running his hands through his hair. It was a move she had seen before.

'Josh does that exact same thing,' she smiled. 'I honestly have no intention of interfering in his life. I have never come on to him, nor have I led him on. I'm not that way inclined. I believe in faithfulness. And I'm certainly not a home wrecker. As for Daniel, I don't know what is going on there. You will need to ask your son. Though there clearly is some kind of issue, because he pelted a football at us earlier that missed our heads by mere inches.'

'If he wanted to hit....'

'I know he could have hit us if he wanted. It was absolutely intentional for the ball to land where it did. Daniel knew exactly what it was too. And now they're having words in the tunnel. I really don't know what's happening.' She put her head in her hands, frustrated.

Dale bear hugged her. She felt tiny in his big arms. She wasn't expecting it, but realised she really needed it. She felt oddly safe and comforted. Nothing else needed to be said. The whistle blew to signal kick off and they both hurried outside to take their seats.

Chapter 18

Danielle couldn't say she paid much attention to the first half of the match. Her head was spinning. Her logical and analytical character traits she relied so heavily on, now eluded her. She was utterly confused. Taylor on the other hand, was having the time of his life. He would sleep well tonight, she thought.

Danielle was jolted out of her musings by Dale and his brother jumping out of their seats and swearing. She looked down to see what the cause of the outburst was, and saw Josh on the floor. She quickly grabbed her tablet and watched the replay to see what happened. She gasped as she watched the opposition's defender, slide tackle him to the ground, completely taking his legs out from under him. Josh landed on his arm at an awkward angle. The camera was on him, still on the ground, clutching his arm and writhing in agony. The defender was pleading his innocence to the referee. He felt Josh had taken a dive and was standing over him, shouting.

Out of nowhere, Alex Perez, the West Ham striker had run over and pushed the shouting defender away from Josh. That got a cheer from the West Ham fans. The defender went to ground dramatically, and more players from both teams were running over to get involved. Pretty much every player was pushing and shoving. The whistle blowing from the referee, was not the deterrent he had hoped for.

Josh was still on the ground and before she knew it, Danielle was stood rooted to the spot watching on. She was terrified that the commotion would spill out and on to his head. Luckily, it seemed Alex had the same concerns as she, because he moved players away, simultaneously shielding Josh.

Josh sat up and Danielle felt a wave of relief go through her. She looked down at Taylor who was teary and worried.

'It's ok baby,' Danielle said, picking him up and cuddling him. 'Josh is tough. He'll get back up.'

And with that, the crowd erupted in applause to Josh standing up, and walking back toward his team bench, holding one hand in the other. Even the opposition fans were clapping for him. He was an England man after all.


Danielle sat back down in her seat. A substitute came on to the pitch to replace Josh, confirming that he was too injured to carry on. She rubbed her eye under her sunglasses and was surprised it was wet. She turned around to see the back of Mr Linberg, as he rushed out of the box and away to his son. Taylor livened up quickly and was back to cheering his team on.

It was half time and West Ham were in the lead by two goals to one. The fifteen-minute pause in play was Danielle's opportunity to take Taylor to the toilet. He had mastered potty training years earlier, but was prone to being over stimulated. He would often be so focussed on what he was doing, forgetting he needed the loo.

The game ended three one to West Ham. Taylor was on a come down as they made their way back to the hospitality suite. Danielle had decided to let the stadium empty out before heading home. She sat and exhausted Taylor on the sofa in the corner of the room and told him to chill with his iPad.

She ordered a large whiskey and was swirling the amber liquid around in her glass, when Josh walked in. His arm was in a sling, but the award-winning smile was back on his face.

'Little one tuckered out?' he said, and nodded towards Taylor.

She turned and saw he was fast asleep. 'It was an eventful game for him. He's very worried about you.'

'Only him?' he said, staring down at Danielle.

'Yup. He likes you. I think you're a giant dick.'

'I *have* a giant dick,' he teased.

Danielle rolled her eyes.

'Plus, if you think I am a giant dick, then why is there mascara all under your eyes?'

She pulled her compact mirror out of her bag and looked at the panda eyed wild woman staring back at her. She snapped it shut and threw it back in to her bag. Great!

'Are you alright?' she asked him. 'What did the doctor say?'

'They think it's probably a fractured ulna. First game back and I'm going to end up injured for six to eight weeks.' He was still trying to look carefree, but Danielle could see the sadness behind his eyes.

He sat down next to her at the table. She could feel the warmth of his body. She was finding it difficult to take her eyes off him. She was so glad he was ok.

He was looking back at her. All traces of a smile gone. His face was serious. His eyes were almost pleading. He wanted her. She could see it all over his face.

She wanted him too. Her mouth watered and she felt an ache between her legs. In that moment all logic and reason were banished. All that remained was primal desire. She was turned on. She wanted to straddle him, kiss him, run her fingers through his hair. She imagined him responding in kind. His working arm pinning her to him. His hand pulling her hair back, so he had easier access to her neck.

No, she thought. He is engaged to another woman, and you are not a home wrecker, she told herself. She picked up the crystal tumbler, and threw back the whisky, concentrating on the burn as it slid down her neck, chasing away any thought of his mouth there.

'That bad huh?' he said. The smile back on his stupid gorgeous face.

She nodded.

'Hear you and my dad had a nice little chat,' he said.

She nodded again.

153

'I'm sorry. He shouldn't have accosted you.'

'Not at all. He actually made a lot of sense. Told me some information I was unaware of too.'

'Oh?' he said, his brows furrowing threatening another angry blow up.

'Yes. Apparently, you're engaged,' she said, looking at the empty glass rather than his face.

'Why do you care? You're clearly getting chummy with Daniel?'

At that moment, her head snapped up to look at him, and Craig walked in.

'Leave us Craig,' Josh commanded

'Actually Craig. Could I please have another?' she said, shaking the empty tumbler.

Craig looked at Josh confused and terrified. Josh nodded and he backed out of the room to fetch her whisky.

'You were saying?' he said, attempting to resume the conversation.

'Nothing.'

Craig came back in with Danielle's drink. He read the room well and said absolutely nothing. He placed her drink down on the table, and removed the empty glass. He retreated and closed the door behind him.

Danielle knocked back the second tumbler almost immediately. She opened her mouth to speak but stopped, when Daniel entered the room. Oh fuck! she thought.

'Hey,' he said, looking directly at her. 'I just want to give you my number. I asked for yours but apparently, I'm not allowed it.'

'Get. Out.' Josh looked at him with such contempt, she thought he might kill him. Sprained ulna or no sprained ulna.

Instead of retreating, Daniel moved forward and set a piece of paper, with his number scrawled on it, in front of Danielle.

'Thank you,' she said, picking the paper up.

Josh watched the exchange that was happening in front of him and left the room.

# Chapter 19

Danielle threw herself on the bed. Josh hadn't come back after he stormed out. Daniel kissed her goodbye and also exited the room. She got out of there as quickly as she could and came home. She dropped a very tired Taylor back to Bradley and took herself back to her house.

She was annoyed. She was confused. She was frustrated. She reflected on the day's events in an attempt to organise her thoughts.

Josh was engaged to Aimee. That fact overruled any other feelings they may or may not have for each other. Sure, there was sexual tension, and Josh had a jealousy issue, but that was his problem. Danielle was single and free to do whatever she liked. And she liked Daniel. He had made it very clear that he liked her too.

She sat up and retrieved the paper he had written his number on from her bag. She programmed it into her phone and sent a message.

She wondered whether to send a message to Josh too. She cared about him, and although they could never happen, she did want them to get on. They worked together after all.

'For fucks sake,' she shouted out loud. This whole thing was making her crazy.

Daniel messaged her back almost instantly. They spent the rest of the night going back and forth, and had agreed to meet for a drink after work on Monday. Danielle asked if they could meet away from the office as she didn't want Josh to see. It was none of his business, but she didn't want to rub his nose in it.

She woke up to a constant buzzing. Ava had called her six times in succession. She sat bolt upright and answered the phone.

'Are mum and dad ok?' she asked, holding her breath and waiting for Ava to answer.

'Yes, they are both fine. I'm calling to ask what the hell is going on with you and Josh?'

'What? What are you talking about?'

'The house phone rang this morning, and it was a journalist trying to get information about you and Josh. Apparently you're having a secret love affair?' Ava blurted out. 'So, I ask again, what's going on?'

'What did you tell them?' Danielle asked.

'I told them that you would never be someone's mistress, that there was no story to tell, and to fuck off.'

'Thank you.'

Danielle didn't feel any relief. She was happy nothing had been said to fuel this journalists fire, but she felt uneasy about someone trying to dig into her personal life. She explained to Ava that nothing was going on, and they were just work colleagues, which was the truth. Danielle wasn't sure Ava believed her entirely, but she was satisfied enough to let her go.

She needed to tell Josh about this. Her intention was to hold off communication until the following day, but this couldn't wait. She decided to text rather than call; *'Are you at the hotel this afternoon or evening?'*

It was to the point. It was exactly how he sent messages to her. She thought it would be best to talk about this face to face, and that would also give her the opportunity to tell Josh about the drink with Daniel.

She left her phone on the bed and got in the shower. She dressed in her cream JL13 sweatshirt and joggers. Technically it was for men, but she liked the feel. Once dressed, she checked her phone to see if he had replied. There were two blue ticks next to the message, confirming that he had read it, but had not responded.

Danielle went downstairs and lazed on the sofa. She had turned on the tv, but she wasn't paying attention to it. She was trying to convince herself that the disappointment she felt was misplaced. Usually, he responded to her immediately after reading her messages. She liked that he was attentive. It made her feel good. She didn't feel good in that moment.

Danielle decided she would just send him another message; *'I assume you're too busy to reply to me today. Wanted to let you know that a journalist called my parents' house today trying to get information about me and suggesting I'm your latest mistress. Thought you should be aware.'*

Once the message had sent, she turned off her phone. She hated herself for constantly checking if he had responded, and turning the phone off meant she would not be able to. She knew the way she had written the message would piss him off. She wouldn't admit it to herself, but she wanted to rile him, so he responded to her.

Danielle arrived at the hotel earlier than usual. She was restless at home and needed a distraction. She was uncomfortable with her own emotions. She shouldn't be spending so much time thinking about Josh. She planned to spend the evening working on her laptop to channel her mind in a more productive manner.

Still in her tracksuit, she walked through the foyer and straight past Josh, who was sitting in the lounge opposite check in. He had his laptop on the table and was tapping away. She pretended she didn't see him. She almost made it to the elevator, before she felt that familiar tingle alerting her to his presence.

'Why are you ignoring me?' he said. He was standing so close behind her, that she could feel his breath on her neck.

'That's rich.' The words were out of her mouth before she had a chance to think. She planned to be indifferent when she next saw him.

The elevator arrived and she walked in. He followed, still very close behind her. A French family laden with suitcases had also joined them in their car, and so it was a tight squeeze. Danielle was first in and stood at the back. By the time the elevator begun its assent, Josh was pushed up against her.

160

Danielle tried to move herself out from him but there was nowhere to move to. She worked hard to ignore her increased heart rate. She hoped he couldn't feel it from his extremely close position. She avoided eye contact and prayed for the French family to get off at a higher level. She didn't want to be left in the car with him alone.

That prayer was answered. A few of them had to step out for her to exit. She did so as quickly as possible and made a beeline for her door. She was quick, but not quick enough. She entered the room and just as the door was closing behind her, Josh used his foot to hold it open.

She continued to ignore him as she sat on her bed. He sat on the bed next to her and laughed. Before she knew what she was doing, she was laughing too. This whole fucked up situation was beyond ridiculous. They sat next to each other laughing for what felt like minutes. Their laughter ended abruptly, when he pulled her chin towards him, and kissed her.

Danielle was powerless to stop him. She had resisted her feelings for him for so long, she had no strength left to deny herself. She kissed him back. She was immediately lost in her lust for him. Her whole body ached with desire.

He manoeuvred himself closer to her and attempted to straddle her, when she put her hand on his chest and pushed him back. He got off the bed and stood in front of her. He grabbed her hand and put it over his heart. She could feel it beating very fast. His beautiful green eyes were staring at her, so intensely, as he held her hand there. He took a step back and pulled her up, so she was stood in front of him. He didn't let go of her hand but dropped it to her side.

Still, he was looking at her. She wanted to break the contact but couldn't bring herself to. It was as if there was some kind of force holding them in place. He leaned in and kissed her again. She lifted her chin, so he had full access to her mouth. He grazed her lip with his teeth and a whimper escaped her. The noise broke the spell and again, she pushed him away. She locked her elbow to ensure there was a distance between them.

'No Josh. We can't. This is wrong,' she said.

He looked like she had slapped him in the face. He stood there for another full minute, then turned and walked out of the room.

'Fuck,' she said to no one but herself.

What was she going to do now? How had she let that happen?

She knew exactly how. She wanted it just as much as he did. She had had dreams about it. She had woken up in the night panting and soaked in sweat. She had even reached for him in her bed and felt utter disappointment when she realised, she was dreaming, and he wasn't there. She waited for her breathing to return to normal, then called the kitchen to order some food. Whilst she was waiting for it to arrive, she turned her phone on.

She felt a flutter when she saw his name flash up on the screen. She opened the message and anticipation turned to unease, *'the reporter won't be bothering you anymore and neither will I. Enjoy your drink with Daniel.'*

## Chapter 20

Danielle was at her desk paying no attention to the report she had open on her screen. Her head was filled with questions that had absolutely nothing to do with JL13. How the hell had Josh found out about Daniel? Did he know before he barged in to her room? If he did, what the hell was he doing? Was he trying to jeopardise any relationship that might form between them?

But why would he do that? No matter how intense and insanely hot that kiss was, he was marrying Aimee. The thought of him doing that made her feel sick to her stomach. How had she ended up in this predicament? She had lost her fucking mind!

'What's got up his nose?' Ginny was stood next to her desk and watched Josh walking towards his office, then closing the door. Danielle looked up just as he frosted the glass walls.

'No idea,' she replied.

Ginny gave her a look as if she didn't quite believe Danielle was unaware of the reason for his hostility, but she didn't pry.

Danielle got out of that building as quickly as possible. Josh was still in there. He hadn't come out of his office since he arrived.

In the taxi on the way to meet Daniel, she was still wondering what Josh was so mad about? She shook her head to stop herself thinking about Josh, and turned her focus to Daniel.

They met in a pub next to the river. The weather was warm, so she ordered a drink and sat out in the beer garden. Daniel arrived twenty minutes late.

'Sorry darling. I couldn't get away,' he said.

He looked like he had just come from the golf course. He was wearing beige chinos and a white polo shirt. He smelt divine. Sitting down at the table, he immediately took her hand and kissed it.

She smiled. She hoped he couldn't see the disappointment behind her eyes. Josh was never late to meet her. Even when she thought he was an egotistical prick, he still turned up on time. Banishing these thoughts away, she took a sip of her drink and said, 'how was your day?'

He continued to hold her hand and told her about his day. They shared wine and chatted about everything and nothing. Daniel was perfectly pleasant, and a real gentleman. She wished the evening had served as more of a distraction. Daniel was good looking, easy to talk to, and gentlemanly.

Danielle loved chivalry. Although she was an independent woman, she loved it when a man pulled out a chair for her. He had asked her several times throughout the evening if she was cold, offering his jacket to keep warm with.

Her head just wasn't in it. She compared everything Daniel did to Josh. There were a number of things that objectively, he was better than Josh at. She had certainly never been offered his coat. But then why would he? It was so frustrating how many times Danielle had to remind herself that Josh was not single. Yes, he had kissed her, but he was not a free agent.

The fact that she couldn't stop thinking about him was enough for her to stop anything developing between her and Daniel. It wasn't fair to him. He was perfectly pleasant, and easy on the eye, he just wasn't Josh.

At the end of their evening, they shared a taxi to take them to their respective hotels. Danielle was first out. She thanked Daniel again for a lovely evening, and kissed him on the cheek. As she did so, he moved his head so that the kiss was on his lips. Before she knew what was happening, Daniel slid his hand up her thigh. He was under her skirt and trying to manoeuvre his hand as high as he could get it. He was trying to force her legs open. Simultaneously, he tried to force his tongue in her mouth.

She tried to pull away, but his grip tightened on her thigh so much that it hurt. His other hand was on the back of her head, holding her in place. He was so strong she couldn't move him. Instead of pulling away, she changed tactics and jerked her head forward, butting her forehead on his as hard as she could. He instantly recoiled and, to her utter shock, he slapped her face. She couldn't believe what was happening.

As soon as he had done it, he apologised and tried to touch her cheek.

'Get the fuck off me now!' Danielle screamed at him. She opened the door and yanked her other hand away from his. The taxi driver got out with her and asked her if she was ok.

'Why are you helping me now that I am out of the fucking car?' she shouted at him. 'Why didn't you intervene when you could see I was trying to pull away from that psycho?'

'Do you know who he is?' the man started, and Danielle held up her hand in disgust.

'Don't you dare. Who he is does not mean he gets away with manhandling women. You're a fucking disgrace.' She turned on her heels and went inside to the safety of the hotel.

Danielle needed a drink. Her face stung and ached when she moved her jaw. She was so shocked and very angry. She took herself to an area of the terrace that wasn't well lit. She didn't want to be alone in that moment, but she didn't want anyone to talk to her either.

Thankfully, the waitress who came to take her order was not Jessica. That would have been the cherry on top of that godawful day. Danielle knew there was no way she would have the self-discipline to stop herself, if that stupid bitch came near.

She ordered a double whiskey on ice and sat quietly watching the other patrons. The group not too far from her were laughing and joking and enjoying each other's company. Danielle couldn't remember the last time she had laughed like that with her friends.

The nice waitress came back with her drink and put it down in front of her.

'Put it on room 725,' Danielle said.

'It's already been paid for madam,' she said.

'By whom?' Danielle asked.

The waitress nodded in the direction of the person who had paid for her drink. It was Josh. She wasn't in the mood. She had no room left to deal with any more shit that day.

She nodded and the waitress retreated. Danielle stared at the swirling amber liquid in her glass. The ice had begun to melt and was trailing a watery line around the edge.

'I'm not in the mood Josh.'

Even in her weakened state, she could still sense the charged air that surrounded her whenever he came near to her. She didn't look up. He sat across from her and said nothing. He was sipping what looked like water, but she didn't raise her eyes to see for sure.

'Nice evening?' he said, looking at the top of her head.

She couldn't deal with this. She lifted her head and gulped back the whisky.

'What the fuck is that on your face?'

His voice was low but sinister. He was beyond angry. Danielle was scared. She didn't answer him.

'Danielle, what the fuck is that on your face?' he said again.

He got out of his chair and reached for her face to take a closer look. She recoiled.

'Look at me,' he said, softer than before but still barely containing anger.

He moved his hand forward again. Slower this time so that she could see it coming. She didn't resist his touch, but kept her eyes on her now empty glass.

Gently, he moved her head up so she would look at him. Reluctantly she did, and he could see the red handprint across her cheek.

'I'm going to fucking kill him,' he said.

He started to pull away and leave. She lifted her hand and grabbed his as it retreated. She put it back where it was.

'Please don't leave me right now,' she said.

Her voice broke slightly, and he moved closer pulling her to him. He gently put her head on his chest and moved his other arm round her. She cried. Not something she ever did in front of people, but the events of the last few days had overwhelmed her.

Josh stroked her hair as held her there gently and firmly. She was vulnerable but unafraid. The way he held her made her feel certain, for that moment at least, everything was going to be ok.

A long while later she lifted her head and felt extremely exposed. People were staring at them. They had definitely recognised Josh. One of them got their phone out and took a picture in full view of them.

Josh made a signal, and two men stood up from a table to the right and grabbed the guy's phone. During the commotion Josh stood and held out his hand for Danielle to take.

'Let's go somewhere a little more private,' he said.

She let him lead her away. Before she knew it, they were at the door to his room. She stopped outside.

'I thought my room would be better as I have a lounge area. That's the only reason we're here.'

She believed him. He poured her another drink and handed it to her. His fingers lingered slightly but he pulled them away before it felt awkward.

'Would you let me put some ice on that?' he asked, and she nodded.

He retrieved an ice pack and wrapped it in a towel before gently placing it on her face. She winced. It was freezing.

'It will take the sting out and reduce the swelling.'

He had been injured enough times to know the drill. She took it from him and held it in place. He sat on the same sofa but at the opposite end. He was near to her but not so close that it could have been interpreted as a come on.

'Can you please tell me what happened?' he asked.

She told him. By the time she had finished, the ice had melted and she put the wet towel on the floor. She looked at him and he was trying to control red hot anger. His hand gripped the corner of the sofa so tightly, his knuckles were white, and she could see all the veins in his arm and hand.

'You're going to do yourself another injury,' she said, nodding towards the hand.

He released and said calmly, 'I want to make him bleed.'

His tone scared her. Not for herself, but for Daniel. She was certain he meant every word.

'I don't want you to do that. Don't get involved.'

'In this situation baby, you don't have any say in how I react.'

He had called her baby. God, she loved that! It sent a warm feeling right through her.

'Would you let me hold you?' he asked.

She couldn't comprehend what was happening. Typically, she was able to read situations objectively. Today, objectivity had eluded her. When it came to Josh Linberg, she was erratic. She actively pushed against logic and reason where he was concerned. Her head and her heart were at constant loggerheads. Danielle prided herself on her strict moral code. It was a core part of who she was. No matter how hard she tried, she could not deny the attraction. Doing so took every morsel of energy.

If she was honest with herself, she wanted him. She wanted to be near to him. Her feelings were undeniable. In the momentary times that she didn't fight, she felt, satisfied, happy, elated. He was a drug to her, and she was addicted. What was it they say?

*'The first step to recovery is acknowledging you have a problem.'*

Maybe it was time to accept that. But this was a really big problem. She didn't want to be the other woman. She wanted to be the centre of his world. She didn't want to share him with anyone.

What right did she have to say that though? He was in a long-term relationship. He was engaged to marry another woman. Did he love Aimee? Did he want to marry her? Was she becoming one of those lovesick girls she usually pitied? She truly felt she wasn't. She saw the way his body responded to her. She felt the passion, the obsession when they shared a kiss. She knew what was behind those intense stares. He didn't flirt with her like he did with other women. He had never winked at her.

The events of the evening had broken down what was left of an already besieged wall. She looked at him and thought he seemed scared for her answer. She didn't answer him. She moved herself so that she was resting on his chest. He put his arm around her, and she held it in place with her hand. He kissed her head but didn't make any more moves. She wanted to stay like this forever. She felt so safe, so warm, so... loved.

## Chapter 21

She opened her eyes and was momentarily disoriented. The sun was beating through the slats in the blind. Fuck. Danielle thought. She had fallen asleep on Josh. She sat up and was reminded about her face by the stinging sensation.

'Ow fuck,' she said, moving her jaw and touching her face.

It was at that moment she felt behind her, and he wasn't there. She stood up and took a look at herself in the mirror on the wall. She couldn't believe the state of her. Still fully clothed from the night before, her hair was crazy. She had puffy eyes from crying and a perfect outline of a handprint on her face. The corner of her lip had a little cut and a purple bruise next to it.

She looked at her watch. It was three in the afternoon. How the fuck had she slept all day? She was supposed to be at work. Well, that wasn't happening. The day was practically over! She found her bag and pulled out her phone.

She had a few messages, but she went straight to the one from Josh, *'I didn't want to wake you. Stay as long as you like. I've told Ginny you're unwell and won't be in. Xx'*

She needed a shower. That was the priority. She put her phone in her bag and made towards the door. As she opened it to leave, Aimee was standing there about to enter.

Great! Danielle thought. This week just keeps getting better and better. Aimee pushed her in an attempt to put her off balance. Her tiny little hand had not moved Danielle an inch.

'What the fuck are you doing here. Where is my fiancé?'

Her face had turn red with anger. She was clearly going for the ferocious Rottweiler, she looked more like scrappy fucking doo! Danielle went to leave again but Aimee put her foot across the door to stop her.

'I do not know what the fuck he sees in you. Look at the state of you. You're hideous,' she said, pointing a finger in Danielle's face. She continued, 'we are getting married next month, and you will not stop that.'

Danielle felt like she had been slapped in the face again. Her whole life was turning into a fucking episode of Eastenders.

'Move out my fucking way,' she said, placing a hand on either shoulder, and shifting Aimee aside with ease.

What was Josh playing at? Getting married next month and pursuing her? Danielle had made the mistake of thinking that she was somehow different from the hundreds of other women, but he must have played them like this too. Enough was enough. She could not handle any more. She showered, changed, and packed to get the fuck out of Walford.

On the way home, she sent messages to Josh, Ginny and Lucy, telling them she would be leaving. She had never been more sure that she should remove herself from a situation.

The previous night, she had talked herself in to believing things could work out for them. That he wasn't in love with Aimee anymore and so could commit to her. She had allowed herself to show vulnerability, and here she was, getting smacked in the face because of it. It could have easily gone so much further. She was weak enough to have done something stupid if he had tried it on. If she was honest with herself, part of her had been disappointed that he didn't,

There was no way she could continue to work for him. How could she respect him now that he had put her in this situation. She had now broken all of her own rules, she had lost respect for *herself*.

More than that, she couldn't watch him marry Aimee. She couldn't pretend to be happy for him. The thought of him dressed in a suit, waiting at the alter for his beautiful bride, made Danielle feel nauseous. She would rather stick pins in her eyes. She would rather stick pins in *his* fucking eyes!

She needed to do some soul searching to reconnect herself She needed perspective. What was she doing getting involved? She was sure it would be his ego, if any that would cross the line. In the end, it was hers. It would take some time for her to come to terms with that. It was a character flaw she didn't realise she had. How stupid could she be?

She asked the taxi at Tunbridge wells to take the long way home because she didn't want to risk seeing anyone in her family. She needed a few days to get her head on straight and she did that best alone.

She thanked the driver, paid him with the cash she had, and entered her house. After she closed the front door, all composure had left her. She slid down the back of the door to the floor and cried.

She stayed there for a long while just staring into nothingness. In the sanctity of her home, she did not need a mask. She allowed the vulnerability to overwhelm her. She allowed her composure to falter.

As the tears subsided, she did some reflecting. She should feel ashamed and embarrassed. She was humiliated. Aimee's words had cut through her like a knife. But if she set aside the guilt, she couldn't bring herself to regret it. She had felt something she hadn't experienced before. That fire, that passion. The all consuming need to be with someone. Yes, she had been a fool, but somehow, it was worth it to experience the emotions.

Eventually she got herself up off of the floor and ran herself a bath. She washed away her shame and confusion and took the time to centre herself. After a soak, she dressed in a fresh pair of pyjamas and pulled her blanket downstairs to the couch.

Her phone had rung several times from her handbag. Danielle had no desire to answer it, no matter who it was. She napped between fits of crying, analysing, and watching crime shows on tv.

She didn't want to know what was going on in the world outside her home. She wanted to cocoon herself in the blanket and go through the motions. She knew she had to, in order to move on. The logical side of her had to be pushed down, whilst she allowed herself to process things. It was new territory for Danielle. She had given advice to friends in the past, but going through it herself, was quite different.

She ordered herself some comfort food. She was unlikely to be able to stomach it, but she knew she needed to try. There was no way she was going to be able to cook in her current state.

Danielle checked on the takeaway's website to track her delivery at the same time she heard her doorbell go. She grabbed her purse and went to the door to collect her food. When she opened it, she was frozen to the spot. It was not the delivery man at the door, it was Josh.

# Chapter 22

'You left this in the office,' he said, handing her the cardigan she kept on the back of her chair.

She didn't move. She couldn't. it was as if her body had been glued to the spot. She just stared at the garment in his outstretched hand. Silent. She took a moment to steady herself and regain control of her faculties.

'Thank you,' she said, and reached out to grab it.

He didn't let it go. She moved her gaze from the cardigan, slowly up to his face. It hurt her to look in his eyes, but she forced herself to do it. After a moment of intense eye contact, she reached out to try again. Still, he held on to it, not letting go.

He dropped the cardigan on the ground and pushed her back in to her hallway. His working hand firmly gripping her arms, he shut the front door and pushed her up against it. He put his nose to hers and stared at her.

The moment was so intense. The air was filled with a dangerous and intoxicating charge. Danielle had never felt so alive. Her nerve endings were exposed, and it felt like she could feel every charged particle brush past her. It was like she had been plunged into an ice bath, gasping for air. She couldn't blink. She didn't want to miss a millisecond.

She could feel his heart racing and hers was too. He was starting to pant as if breathing was becoming difficult. Not getting closer to each other was causing them both physical pain. Danielle couldn't take it.

She moved her face, so her lips were in line with his and kissed him. In that moment she didn't care about anything other than getting as close as possible to the man in front of her. He let go of her arms and she wrapped them round his neck. Her fingers were in his hair, pulling his head down and holding him to her, as she slid her tongue in his mouth. With each lick of her tongue, he returned in kind.

He let out a low groan and Danielle felt it reverberate through her. She was so turned on she thought he could make her come just by kissing her. His hands slid down her back and beneath the band of her pyjama bottoms. She wasn't wearing any underwear. Josh had realised this and groaned again as he kneaded her arse. He pulled her away from the door and set her down gently on the stairs. They were so desperate for each other, so hungry and greedy, there was no way they would make it to the bedroom.

He pulled at her trousers and threw them behind him, returning his hand to her arse. He pushed his body closer to hers, forcing her legs to widen. His hand moved to her front and stroked the opening of her pussy.

'Oh baby, you are so wet for me,' he said into her mouth, as he continued kissing her desperately.

Her hips arched up in response to his touch and she let out a little moan of her own. His fingers were probing deeper. He attempted to use his teeth to undo her pyjama top. He only had the use of one hand and that was being put to better use. She took over for him using her own hands to undo her top. She undid the last button and her top fell open, freeing her braless tits.

'Fuck.' He breathed. He took a temporary reprieve from kissing her to admire her body. 'Baby you are beautiful,' he said.

His eyes darkened as his lust increased. He kissed and sucked on her neck greedily as he worked his way downward. Her nipples were so hard. She jerked in glorious pain when he used the tip of his tongue to flick them. She moaned and writhed, desperate for him to take her. She tugged at his t shirt and pulled it over his head, throwing it in the

184

general direction of her trousers. His mouth moving down further, she took the opportunity to free herself entirely from her top.

His kisses reached the top of her cleft. She was panting, impatient to feel his tongue. Simultaneously, he entered her with his fingers and ran his tongue over her clit. She was so sensitive her body bucked uncontrollably. Josh didn't slow down. Instead, he took her inability to control herself as an invitation to bring her soaring into her first orgasm. She was so desperate and turned on, she gripped on to the banister to steady herself.

The after shocks of her orgasm were soaring through her, causing her to try and pull back for some relief. Josh lifted her legs and put them either side of his head, so they were resting on his shoulders. He had masterfully worked his tongue to drop the intensity, so her orgasm could build up again. The temporary reprieve was short lived when he again, upped the tempo, and the feeling intensified again.

This time, she grabbed at his hair and was pulling him into her, as she used her hips to greedily guide him where she wanted. The result was an even more powerful sensation washing over her body. She looked down just as he looked up at her. The need in his eyes bore in to her and sent her off again into an orgasm that had her shouting out her pleasure.

'Please,' she panted, as she slowly came back down to earth. She pulled his head back by his hair.

'I've been wanting to do that to you for two months,' he said.

His voice was low, and his eyes were dark. He was looking from her face to her body and back again. Even that felt sexual. It was primal desire. Their bodies were so desperate for each other. It was more powerful than anything she had ever experienced before.

'My turn,' she said, through panting breaths.

She hoisted herself up on to her elbows, paying no attention to the pain she felt from friction burns with the carpet.

'Stand up,' she told him.

He looked at her with a wicked smile but did as he was told. She took a moment to take in him standing there in a pair of tracksuit bottoms and a bare chest. His mouth still wet with her orgasm, she stood up and kissed him. She could feel his big hard bulge on her belly. She got on to her knees and pulled at his waist band, freeing his beautiful cock.

'Mmm,' she said, as she ran her tongue along the length of him.

'Fuck,' he said, looking down at her.

Seeing how turned on he was from the sight of her eye level with his cock thrilled her. She licked and kissed him up and down his impressive length, then hollowed her cheeks to take him in with her mouth.

'Oh baby,' he growled.

He was pushing himself in a little at a time. She watched him as he did. His eyes were closed as he concentrated on the feeling. She cupped his balls and ran her teeth lightly over his helmet, licking his opening as she did so. His legs shook. She released his balls, and used her hand to pump him from base to tip. Her mouth working in tandem as she did so.

He grabbed her ponytail pulling her away, and upward so they were both standing. Without letting go of her hair, he pulled at it again, so her head went back, and her neck was exposed. He kissed her open mouthed from her earlobe to the base of her neck. He released her hair and pushed her back gently but firmly, so her back was resting on the stairs.

Pausing for a moment, their greedy and desperate eyes locked, both were anticipating the next part. He didn't break the stare when he put his knees on the bottom step and angled himself into position. He was panting in anticipation, and she was biting down on her bottom lip, desperate to feel him. When he saw her do it, he reached his limit, and pushed himself in to her.

Danielle could not describe the feeling if she tried a thousand times. It was ecstasy. The feeling was worth the wait. He leant down and kissed her greedily. She responded in kind. She took the change in position to grab hold if his arse and pull him into her. Her hips were thrashing upward, and his were pushing him in. It was wild, it was clumsy, it was roar. They were both lost in achieving the height of their pleasure.

His pace quickened and he started to shake. She wrapped her legs around him pulling him in. He made noises that called her body to give him everything he needed. He dropped his head grunting and panting.

'Look at me,' she said, pulling his head up gently.

She wanted to see him lose control. She needed to see it to reach her own euphoric height. They were looking at each other, both reaching a new level of pleasure from watching the other, and came.

They stayed in that position for a while absorbing each other's aftershocks, clinging on to each other tightly. Josh sagged into her, completely drained mentally, physically and emotionally.

They laid there, unable and unwilling to move for a long while. He stroked her hair, and she nuzzled into his neck inhaling him.

Their heart rhythm had almost returned to normal when Danielle said, 'what now?'

# Chapter 23

'I'm thinking we rest for ten minutes then do that again,' he said smiling.

Danielle gave a weak laugh. 'We need to talk.'

'Do we?' he said.

'Don't we?' she replied, and raised an eyebrow.

A knot had formed in her stomach, and she felt an overwhelming and unmistakable sense of guilt. What had she done? Who had she become? She felt the urge to be sick. Breaking free of their embrace, she picked up her clothes and redressed herself. She then picked up his clothes and handed them to him. Josh looked confused, and hurt. They had gone from being so close to each other, to feeling miles apart in an instant.

'Where is the bathroom?' he asked her, avoiding her eyes.

'First door on the right.'

He stood and went up the stairs, clothes in hand. She watched him go. His bare arse, gloriously tightening with each step he took. He was so intoxicating. She could smell him all over her. She traced her hand over her neck and downward where he had kissed her.

'Fuck,' Danielle uttered almost inaudibly.

Her moral code was at war with her lust for, and connection to that man. She knew she should feel ashamed but the strength of their pull to each other was undeniable. It was like magnets, they were drawn to one and other.

She went to the kitchen and poured herself a large glass of Malbec. She didn't know if Josh drank red wine, but poured him one too. He came down the stairs as she was heading into the lounge.

He stopped in front of her. She looked at him with tears in her eyes. It physically hurt to be near him. He reached out and gently stroked her face with the back of his hand. She was powerless to stop him. She didn't want to stop him. She wanted him to hold her, to make everything ok. She closed her eyes and concentrated on her breathing. In and out. In and out.

'One of those for me?' he asked, pointing to the wine.

She handed him a glass and he took it with his working hand. They were staring at each other again. Danielle was struggling to think logically. Thankfully, she was thrust back into reality by a knock at the door.

'Take this and go in the lounge for me please,' she said to Josh.

He nodded and did as she asked, whilst she went to open the door. It was the delivery driver who had her Chinese takeaway in one hand, and her purse in the other. She had completely forgotten about both.

'Thank you,' she said.

She took both items from him. She opened her purse, took out a twenty and handed it to him. She felt a reward was necessary. He could have easily taken her purse, and she definitely would not have noticed until it was long gone.

'Too much,' he said, trying to hand it back to her.

She insisted, and he thanked her. She closed the door and went back to the living room.

'I thought you were my food.' She held up the bag and he smiled. It was a wicked smile, and she knew exactly what he was thinking.

She fetched some plates and cutlery, and they sat on the floor, eating and drinking their wine.

As if reading her mind, he said, 'I ended things with Aimee the night of the launch.'

Relief ran through her, instantly de-knotting her stomach. She could feel her body unfurling. She hadn't realised she was so tense.

'Ok,' she managed.

'You wanted to know what I said to her that night. I told her I thought she was disgusting for saying that about you, and that it was the last straw for me. Her personality had changed so much over the last six months.'

He paused and took a sip of his wine. Danielle was taking this all in, unable to speak.

'We had a conversation the next morning when she had sobered up, and I confirmed that the relationship had run its course.'

'How did she take it?' Danielle asked, finding her voice.

'Not well,' he said.

'Why didn't you tell me you'd split two weeks ago?'

If she had known that, she would not have entertained a date with Daniel.

'I wasn't sure if you liked me too until that day in my box,' he carried on, 'the feelings I had were intensifying so quickly, I was trying to make sense of it myself.'

'She came to your room earlier and told me you were getting married next month.'

'She did what?'

'She was at the door as I was leaving. She shouted at me, threatened me, and told me you were getting married next month. That's why I left, and why I quit.'

They sat in silence for a while. Danielle picked at her food, but she was too wired to eat.

'How is your arm?' she said, sensing a change in topic was needed.

'Hurts like a bitch,' he said.

She shuffled closer to him and kissed his fingers. It was a real intimate and vulnerable moment.

194

'I like this look on you,' he teased. 'Am I peeling back a prickly outer layer?'

She lightly bit him by way of a response.

'Ouch.'

Josh pulled his hand away in mock pain. He touched her face again and resumed the intense staring. She was lost. Before she had time to think about it, she had straddled him. Her body was acting independently. He kissed her softly.

He teased her lips apart with his tongue and deepened the kiss. Her heart was racing, her cheeks coloured, and her nipples hardened. She was rocking in time with the kisses. He was hard again. She could feel it through both of their clothes. She had no control. She normally played a lot harder to get, but then she had never been in a situation like this before.

Her hands worked to position him and allow enough room for her to pull his trousers down. She did the same with her own until they were skin to skin. She continued to simulate riding him, teasing him until he was rock solid and panting. Abruptly, he grabbed her and pinned her to him. He adjusted her hips and pushed himself up and into her. She cried out.

Josh let out a moan that sent a shock through her body. That noise was so erotic. She loved that she could make him sound like that. She rose up so just the tip of him remained inside her, then pushed back down, eager to hear him moan again. She got what she wanted and continued the movement, both were watching each other's reaction.

She rose up and dropped down again, but this time he held her there. His hand on her hip, he used his nose to nudge her for a kiss. She complied. The kissing intensified, and she began to struggle against his grip.

'Do as you're told,' he growled through kisses.

She liked it. She loved a man that took control in the bedroom. She loved what *this* man was doing. She tensed and squeezed him with her sex, causing his eye to widen. Seeing him like that made her writhe in place.

'Just like that baby,' he said.

She continued unable to stop. She quickened her pace, and he pushed his pelvis up, filling her entirely. They climaxed together, lost in each other.

They had sex twice more that evening. Once in the shower, and again before they went to bed. Danielle was so exhausted after the last of seven orgasms, she was barely able to move, and fell into a deep sleep.

## Chapter 24

The next morning, they were awoken by a loud knock at the door.

'Danielle love, it's dad.' He let himself in and was halfway up the stairs when she came bursting out of the bedroom in her robe.

'Dad,' she said, as she saw him at the top of the stairs. 'What are you doing here?'

Mr Cooper must have sensed that she may not be alone, as he retreated, taking steps backward until he reached the bottom.

'Your mother and sister are frantic. You haven't answered your calls or messages for twenty-four hours. They thought you were dead!' he said.

'So dramatic.'

'I thought so too at first, but then Ava called the office and was told you didn't arrive, and that you hadn't shown up for work. A family emergency apparently. What the hell is going on?'

She followed him into the kitchen and sat down at the breakfast bar. He filled the kettle with fresh water.

'I'm sorry dad. I have had a crazy few days, and I just wanted to shut the world out whilst I dealt with it.'

'Not good enough young lady. If I go back to your mother with that explanation, it will be me who's dead.'

She started to answer when her dad's wide stare stopped her. She turned to see what he was looking at, and rolled her eyes dramatically.

'I'm sorry Mr Cooper. It's my fault she has been out of contact.' Josh made his way to the breakfast bar and sat down on the stool next to Danielle.

Fuck! She thought. What the hell did she do now? What if she wasn't ready to tell her family? Had he considered that? She didn't even know what it was they were doing. Well, she knew they had mind-blowing, earth-shattering sex last night, but they hadn't spoken about labelling it.

Mr Cooper looked from Danielle to Josh for a long while. His mouth moved a couple of times, but no words came out.

Eventually, he settled on, 'I'm not actually sure what to say.'

He rubbed his slightly wet hands from filling the kettle on a tea towel, and offered his hand to Josh.

'Nice to meet you,' he said.

Danielle imagined the battle that must be going on in her father's head. Josh was a West Ham legend. He was also the man he found in his daughter's house after twenty-four hours of radio silence. Mr Cooper added another cup to the two that were awaiting a boiling kettle, and was about to speak again when his phone rang.

'It's your mum,' he said. 'I'll take this in the garden.'

Mr Cooper left the room and Danielle punched Josh in his good arm.

'Ouch,' he said, rubbing the spot she had just hit. 'What's that for?'

'What if I didn't want my dad, and in about five minutes my whole family to know about us,' she said. 'Not that I even know what *us* is.'

'What do you mean you don't know what *us* is?' He looked hurt. 'I thought it was pretty clear what we were after last night. Maybe it meant something different to you.'

'No. It meant a lot to me. I just wasn't sure if it was a one-time thing or,' she stopped speaking.

He stood from the chair and walked out. She heard him go back upstairs and close the bedroom door. She was about to get up and go after him when her dad came back in.

'Your mother is mad at you,' he said, shaking the phone at her.

'I'm really sorry dad. I just completely lost track of time.'

'It's ok darling. You know what your mother is like, she worries.'

'I'm a fucking adult,' she started, but seeing the look on her dad's face, she softened and relented. 'I'm sorry. I should have told you guys I was at home.'

'So, you've quit your job?' he asked, trying to keep his face impassive. 'Is that because of.' He pointed at the empty chair next to her where Josh had been.

'Actually no. I quit first, then that happened,' she said, also pointing at the empty chair.

'I have clearly walked in on something, so I am going to leave the coffee and head home. I need to stop your mother from marching round here herself.'

'Ok dad. I will call her this evening and explain.'

With that, Mr Cooper planted a kiss on the top of his daughter's head and left. Danielle wished she didn't swear at him. Her nerves were on edge, and she was still so God damned tired. She made a move towards the stairs when she saw Josh had started to come down.

Before she said anything he said, 'I'll be off then.'

'What?' she said, confused.

'If you think that last night was a one off, then there is no need for me to still be here.'

He wouldn't look at her. He chose instead to look at the floor. He got to the bottom step, and she put a hand on his chest to stop him. She knew he didn't really want to leave by how easy it was to stop him. She didn't know what to say. This was all happening so fast, and she had had so many emotions in the last twenty-four hours.

Utter devastation when Amy told her they were getting married next month. Despair when she got back home and was able to let her emotions go. Confusion when she tried to sort through her feelings and process what had happened. Surprise when she opened her door expecting the Chinese takeaway and seeing Josh.

Then there was the most dominant and prolific feeling of them all, elation. When he pinned her up against the back of her door, she was filled with eager anticipation. She gave herself to him so wholly and that felt, well, amazing. To be in his arms, to lay on his chest, for him to be all over her, and inside her. He possessed her, and she him. That wasn't a one-time thing. There was an inexplicable bond that bound them together. She had never felt anything close to this before.

She didn't trust herself. She couldn't be sure, because she had never been in a situation where her heart ruled her head. *She* didn't lose control. And so, she was back to confusion, and that's what came bursting out of her when she had spoken to Josh at the breakfast bar. All she knew now was, the thought of him walking out and leaving, filled her with anxiety and dread.

'Please don't go. Stay and talk to me.'

She realised she was staring at her hand on his chest, too scared to look at his face, in case he saw her need.

He had noticed she wasn't looking at him, so he put one finger under her chin, and lifted her head. The action had become familiar.

'Ok,' he said. 'Let's talk'.

They sat at the breakfast bar drinking coffee and discussing what this meant for both of them. Danielle fought past her internal warning sirens and told him how she felt. She was relieved to hear he felt the same. She knew they must. She had been in relationships for years at a time, and had never felt a connection like this. It was so intimate and demanding.

The cat was well and truly out of the bag with her family, but they agreed not to tell anyone else. They needed to get to know each other before facing the outside world as a couple.

'*Couple*.' Danielle couldn't get her head round that word. She couldn't stand him two weeks ago, and now she couldn't stand the thought of being without him. She had to be ok to let him in. He had already stuck his foot in the door, metaphorically and physically.

She sent a quick text to her dad to ask if he could arrange for her siblings to meet at the Cooper house that evening. She asked if they could all be on their own, and not with their other halves. Ideally, she would not be doing this for a few months, but she knew her mum would not be able to keep it quiet, and at least this way she could set the boundaries and control this thing.

She worried about Ella. She knew Casey couldn't keep it from her. They were married after all. She just hoped that there was some decency somewhere in her, and she would keep her big mouth shut. She was momentarily sad that she didn't have a good relationship with Ella. She and her brother were so close. Danielle would love to have a relationship with her sister-in-law. Unfortunately, this sister-in-law, was a self-obsessed, jumped-up, little bitch!

Danielle wondered whether to raise the topic that burned her. She was worried how he would take it. They had agreed to get it all out, so she braced herself on the edge of the table and said, 'Aimee.'

'Yeah,' he said, looking at her quizzically.

'Two things. Your dad already told me that your mum and sister love Aimee and therefore, do not like me.'

He went to speak but she held her hand up and continued, 'we could hate each other by next week, so it isn't an imminent problem, I just need you to know that up front. Your sister is best friends with her.'

She left that hanging for a moment, not wanting to add anything more.

'And the second?' he said.

'Do not get shitty when I say this because I have to voice it ok?'

He nodded slowly.

'I am a one-man woman.' She ignored the change in his expression and continued. 'I don't share, and I don't tolerate cheating. Cheating to me includes messaging other women. To clarify, I don't mean messaging friends and family, I mean responding to randomers on Instagram, or women who are looking for a hook up over text. And I don't like the cheeky winks to receptionists and barmaids.' She stopped speaking and waited for him to respond.

'How can you think that I would do that? Haven't I proven already that I'm all in with you. You are all I've thought about since the day I met you.'

'And I love hearing that, but I don't need to point out, that you were with Aimee when you had those feelings.'

He scoffed, but didn't say anything more.

'I know you feel differently about me, I am just saying, whether it's next week or years down the line, I won't have it. We will be done.'

'Anything else?' he said, exasperated.

'Yes,' she said as he rolled his eyes. 'Take me to bed.'

They spent the rest of the day in bed sleeping, watching films, and exploring each other's bodies. Her dad had messaged her back to confirm he had arranged the meet up for seven. Josh was completely unphased at the prospect of meeting her entire family, after being together for the grand total of twenty-four hours.

She had given him a brief overview of each individual. She got to her mum last because she knew her mum would be the unpredictable one. Her dad and brothers already loved him. God knows how Casey was going to be. Her sister would be able to see Danielle was happy and so would be fine. Her mum was still angry at her being out of touch and making her worry. She also knew Josh had a reputation. She read the gossip column in her daily newspaper. She would be worried about her daughter and will take some time to come around.

Josh listened, but was much more interested in trailing kisses down her body. She gave up talking when he reached her naval, and her mind turned to other things.

## Chapter 25

Danielle managed to check her phone in the five minutes she was on the toilet. She had fifteen missed calls from Ginny and six texts. The last one demanded a call back under pain of death. She had thirty, yes, thirty missed calls from her mum. She listened to the first two voicemails she had left, but decided to delete the rest on mass. Her sister had messaged, firstly on her mum's behalf, but the more time that passed, she could read the change in tone.

Finally, she had two missed calls from an unknown number, and one voicemail that was left only thirty minutes earlier. She listened to a high pitch female voice, and was a little shocked to hear the abuse that was coming at her.

'I know you're together somewhere. I just want you to know, he is mine. I've been through this before and he always comes back to me. An ugly fat whore like you won't hold his interest, so get it whilst you can.'

Danielle laughed. She was incredulous and laughing seemed to be the only way to deal with it. She pondered whether to tell Josh. She had decided not to when she heard Josh outside the door, asking what she was laughing at.

Great! She thought. Drama already! She could tell this was not going to be the only time Aimee would be attacking her. It would certainly be the last time she took it without retaliation.

She came out of the toilet and handed him her phone by way of an answer. The smile dropped off his face pretty quickly, and he physically cringed when Aimee called her an ugly, fat whore.

He threw her phone on the bed and made strides toward the bedside table where his phone was charging. Danielle chased after him trying and failing to take his phone away from him.

'Josh. Don't. Just ignore her.'

She stood in front of him trying to make him look at her. He was purposefully avoiding her eyes as he scrolled through his contacts.

They were both startled by a knock at the front door. She had never been so popular. Josh threw his phone on the bed, and ran down the stairs to open the door, telling her it was for him.

She was confused, but took the momentary distraction as her opportunity to hide his phone. He came back into the room with a small holdall in his hand.

'Thought I'd better wear fresh boxers to meet your mum,' he said by way of an explanation. 'Where's my phone?'

'Can you not just forget about the fucking phone and model those boxers for me?'

He raised his eyebrows at her, but did as she asked. Seeing him in all his crowning glory, made Danielle make sure he was no longer thinking about Aimee, or his phone.

They took the short trip to her parent's house and were walking up the driveway by six thirty. Danielle wanted to get there first, so she could speak with her mother before her brothers arrived.

Josh commented on the house, and she gave her stock response. She knocked and put her key in the lock, just as her mum pulled open the door.

She must have been waiting for her to arrive. Daphne threw her arms round her daughter and hugged her tightly. For a small woman, Danielle's mum was very strong. She couldn't breathe.

Knowing better than to comment, she waited for her mum to release her. She soon did, and then she launched into her. All of this before they had crossed the threshold.

'I'm sorry mum. I really am. I won't do it again.' She took her admonishment. 'Could we please come in now?'

Daphne had clearly forgotten that Josh was there until that moment. She allowed them both to enter and led them through to the back patio. She had set the large round table with glasses. In the centre were two coolers. One holding wine and the other, beer. Josh remained standing as Danielle took a seat.

'Shit!' she said, earning herself an evil. 'Mum this is Josh. Josh this is my mum, Daphne.'

'Hello Mrs Cooper,' he said, smiling and held out his hand for her to shake.

Danielle was dumbfounded when her mum shooed his hand away and opened her arms for a hug. Josh winked at Danielle as he returned the hug. He repeated the apology he had given her dad, blaming himself for her being out of touch.

'Please, take a seat. What would you like to drink? Beer, wine, tea, water?'

Josh sat down next to Danielle and asked if he could have a beer. He put a hand on her thigh under the table, and she instantly fizzed. He must have sensed her response, because he moved his hand further up her leg, whilst having a conversation with her mum, completely straight faced. She stood on his foot, hard, and he moved his hand back down to a respectable position.

Her mum asked about his arm and told him how much Taylor hadn't stopped talking about the weekend. Danielle couldn't believe that was only four days ago. So much had happened in such a short space of time.

Her dad and Ava came out together holding bowls of crisps and pretzels. They set them down on the table. Josh rose to shake Mr Coopers hand.

'Ava, this is Josh. Josh, my little sister, Ava.'

He stood up and planted a kiss on her cheek. Ava blushed. Danielle didn't think she had ever seen her blush in her whole life.

213

'I told my husband Derek, to stay out for a drink after work this evening. Apparently, we were to come to this meeting alone,' Ava said.

Danielle was pretty sure Josh was using his powers in female seduction on her mum and sister to charm them in to liking him. She was fine with it. As long as it worked.

Bradley and Casey arrived together with a little addition.

'Josh,' Taylor shouted, and ran to him giving him a big cuddle.

'Hello mate,' he said, hugging him back.

'Looks like neither of us are favourites anymore,' Danielle said to Ava.

'Sorry sis,' Bradley said, 'Gemma had to work late.'

'No worries. I wanted you to meet Josh together. Taylor is already familiar,' she said.

Josh shook both their hands and reseated himself, Taylor instantly jumped on his lap. Danielle was surprised by Casey. She thought he would have been much more excitable.

'Come and sit next to me Casey love,' their mum said, patting the chair next to her.

Danielle now understood why he wasn't excitable. Their mum had given him warning and told him how he was to behave.

They were all settled round the table drinks in hand and making small talk. Danielle seized the opportunity to start talking. She explained that she and Josh were an item, but that it was very new and that they were keeping it secret. She drilled home that this was not something to be discussed outside the house. All agreed, she changed the subject.

'Heard you got caught in the act by dad,' Casey said, he couldn't help himself. That comment earned him a jab to the ribs from Daphne.

'Which bright spark told him that?' Danielle was eying her siblings.

Ava lowered her head providing Danielle with the answer.

'Want to see my bar?' Mr cooper stood up, ending the conversation and ushering Josh and her brothers to the bar.

Danielle felt a sense of relief that it was done. She chatted with her mum and sister about work and what she was going to do now. If she was honest, she hadn't even thought about work.

Ginny. She remembered and stood from the table telling her mum and sister she would be back in a minute. She went to the bar where she found the boys all watching Manchester United play against some Italian team. She walked over to Josh, who was still being smothered by Taylor, and asked if she could borrow him for a moment.

'Come here mate,' Bradley said, and Taylor reluctantly went to his dad.

She led Josh up the stairs to the pantry. She was momentarily startled by Josh grabbing her round the waist and kissing her. She was instantly lost in him. Her hands were round his neck and she wished they were back at her house, alone.

'You're insatiable,' she said. She pulled away, but grabbed his hands, placing them back around her waist.

'Ginny,' she blurted, desperate to stay on topic.

'What about her?'

'I had had missed calls and messages from her all through yesterday and today. I know we said we weren't going to tell anyone, but I do trust her and feel like she deserves an explanation for my sudden departure.'

'That doesn't matter anymore because you're coming back.'

She looked at him confused, 'no, I'm not. I gave my notice.'

'But you don't have the same concerns now, so you can come back.'

'If anything, my concerns are worse,' she said, still not letting him take his hands away. 'We can talk about this later. Can I tell Ginny?'

He smiled at this. 'Yeah. I don't care who you tell. It's you that wants the secret.'

She rubbed her nose on his and let his hands go.

'Better go back downstairs to your little fan club.'

'I prefer *this* fan club,' he said taking a step back and heading for the stairs.

217

Danielle went into the lounge and called Ginny who answered on the first ring.

'What the actual FUCK is going on?'

'Hello to you too!'

'Don't hello me. What is going on? You left me! You left me a shitty little email and vanished. I assume Josh is with you.'

'What?' she said, taken aback by her accurate assumption.

'Josh. You know. Tall blonde handsome fella that you can't stand.' She clipped and continued. 'He came into the office yesterday afternoon, happy as Larry, then charged out snatching your cardigan and leaving. So, I repeat, what is going on.'

Danielle told her everything. When she had finished, there was silence on the other end. After a full minute she heard, 'Well fuck me.'

Danielle laughed. So did Ginny. It was at that moment the doorbell went. She wondered who would be coming over at this time of the evening when they were all already here. It couldn't be Derek because he had a key.

'Listen mate. I have to go. We'll get lunch in a couple of days?'

'Sounds good to me. I still have soooooo many questions.'

'Great. Oh, and Ginny, this is top secret so please don't tell anyone.'

'Scouts honour,' she said, and hung up the phone.

## Chapter 26

Danielle went back outside to ask who was at the door. She realised she didn't need to as Ella was sitting at the table, pouring herself a glass of wine.

'Hi Ella,' Danielle said, trying and failing to produce a genuine smile.

'Oh, now you want to talk to me,' Ella said.

'Not really, no, but as usual you are poking your oar in.'

'Don't fucking talk to me like that. You excluded me on purpose to keep me away from Josh. Worried I would steal him away?' Ella was now out of her seat, voice raised.

'What's going on?' It was Bradley.

'Keep Taylor inside and close the back door for me, will you?' Danielle said. She gave him a look that he had seen a thousand times growing up. He knew to do as she had asked.

When she heard the door shut, she sat at the table. She maintained eye contact with Ella, who had remained standing.

'Shall we ask him what he thinks about you? I don't think you are going to like the answer.' Danielle's voice remained calm and even.

'Don't patrionise me,' Ella said.

Danielle had to fight her very strong urge to correct her. The fact Ella didn't know how to pronounce patronise, was too much.

'Tell me what your actual problem is,' she asked.

'You're my problem. Casey is my husband. We are a couple. It's rude to ask him for a chat and not me.'

'I'm sorry you feel that way. He is my brother, and I wanted to speak with him first, before speaking with you.'

'Fuck off Danielle, you are excluding me on purpose just to be spiteful. You have never liked me. Well I don't like you either you fat cunt.'

Ava stood up, and Danielle told her to go inside and help their mum.

'Do it,' Danielle said. Ava did as she was asked, reluctantly and whilst continuing to stare at Ella in disgust.

It was now just the two of them at the table. Danielle remained seated, whilst Ella was standing, wine glass in hand.

'Don't talk to me like that Ella. Like you said, you are my brother's wife, which unfortunately, makes you family.'

'Fuck right off. You really are a smug fat cunt,' Ella said. She was shaking with rage.

Danielle stared at her deciding what her next course of action should be. She was finding it more and more difficult to maintain her cool. Ella was going for the throat and Danielle really wanted to let her have it.

'His girlfriend is so much more attractive than you,' Ella said, breaking the silence. 'I don't know what kind of witchy shit you have done to make him like you, but it won't last. There are sooo many girls in the queue, waiting for an opportunity to suck his dick.'

It was at this point Danielle had decided she would give it both barrels. She remained in her chair wanting to show Ella that she wasn't intimidated by her.

'It is a lovely dick to suck. I would definitely recommend it. Although I'm not really the sharing type, so you will have to fight me for it,' Danielle said smirking.

Ella's cheeks coloured slightly, and Danielle enjoyed making her blush. She continued, 'listen to me you pathetic, ignorant, moron. I don't really care what you think about me, or my relationship. I have the right to speak to my brother whenever I like. The reason I had to do it privately, was because I needed some advice on how to make sure you kept your big fake mouth shut.'

Ella responded by shouting a load of abuse that caught the attention of the entire household. Everyone came running out just in time to see her launch her glass at Danielle. She moved out of the way and the glass smashed into hundreds of pieces.

'You smug fat cunt,' she repeated.

'Yep, I've heard that one already you fucking idiot.' Danielle smirked again, knowing the reaction she would get from Ella.

True to form, Ella launched herself over the table towards Danielle. Josh had seen it coming and reacted quickly, grabbing the back of Danielle's chair and pulling it back. Ella fell to the ground still screaming like a wild animal. Casey walked over to her and picked her up. He put her over his shoulder, and marched her out of the house.

As they were leaving, Danielle managed to catch Ella's eye and gave her a little wave. She knew she was being petty, but she couldn't help herself.

'Are your family gatherings normally like this?' Josh asked, smiling.

'She's just off her fucking rocker,' Danielle replied.

She was still calmer than she had expected. She surprised herself. Usually, she would retaliate in kind to anyone that spoke to her that way. Hell, she would have welcomed the opportunity to slap the snarl off Ella's heavily make-upped face. She supposed she held her temper because she didn't want to upset her brother.

'She ain't welcome in this house anymore,' Ava said. Now *she* was angry. surprisingly, so was her mum.

Daphne usually worked really hard to keep the peace in her family. Ella and Ava had fallen out on a number of occasions, but her mum had always smoothed it over.

'Why is Casey carrying Ella up the driveway?' Derek had walked in to the aftermath. 'Is that glass on the floor?'

'Yes. Our lovely sister-in-law tried to throw it at my head,' Danielle said matter of factly.

'She did not!' Bradley said. 'What set her off this time.'

'Her nose was put out of joint because she wasn't invited this evening,' Danielle said. 'Can we all take a moment to acknowledge how Derek and Gemma had no issues.' She paused and nodded towards Derek.

'She then went on to tell me I am a witch and have somehow put Josh under a spell, because there was no way he would be interested in a smug fat cunt like me,' Danielle continued. 'Oh, and then she said he would quickly get bored of me, and he had a long line of much slimmer women waiting for the opportunity to suck his dick.'

'Danielle!' Her mum was disgusted.

'I'm just repeating what she said mother.'

The argument signalled the end of the evening. Danielle offered to assist her mum with the clean-up, but Ava insisted she would help.

They walked home in silence. Josh wasn't sure what to say. Danielle was wondering whether what Ella said was true and she was living in a fantasy land. It was the second time she had heard the very same sentiment in one singular evening. Maybe she had no business starting a relationship with a man who could literally have whoever he wanted. She had never doubted herself before, but then she had never been with a man like Josh.

He must have sensed her mind reeling because he grabbed her hand and kissed it.

'Do not let that psycho bitch get in your head.'

'OK.'

'Look at me,' he said, stopping abruptly to stare at her. 'Look at me,' he repeated.

'You are beautiful. Stunning. I have never been more attracted to a woman in my life. And I've been around a LOT of women.'

She laughed. Couldn't help herself. He kissed her head and led her inside the house.

'Let me show you how attractive you are,' he said, pulling her in for a kiss.

# Chapter 27

The next morning Josh had to get up very early and make his way to the training ground. He had to have X-rays on his arm now that the swelling had gone down. He also had a meeting with his manager to discuss his physio schedule.

Danielle felt extremely lonely when she woke up and he wasn't there. She had slept alone in this very bed for years and never felt lonely before. Now she was pining for a man who had stayed over the grand total of two nights.

She pulled herself together and got herself ready for the day. When she was cleaning her teeth, she noticed his electric toothbrush was resting on the side, charging. She smiled at what that signified. He was planning to come back.

She spent the morning looking at the list of prospects she had amassed whilst working for JL13. She knew a few of them would have already filled the position, but there were some that were still looking.

She was doing some research on one of the potentials when her phone rang. It was Casey. He had sent her a text the night before, but she didn't respond. She'd had enough for one day.

'Hey,' she answered.

'What the fuck happened last night sis? Ella said you coaxed her in to doing that so she would look bad.'

'And what do you think?' she said, throwing the question back at him.

'I dunno sis. I've not seen her like that for a long time.'

'Casey, why don't you call me back once you have got your thoughts straight. I am not going to justify my actions, or defend myself from that psychotic wife of yours. You do remember her throwing a glass, and hurling her body at me? How about you ask her to justify that!'

She hung up. He called again and she sent him to voicemail. He called a third time, and she let it ring out. She'd deal with him later.

She arranged a meeting with two companies that she liked the look of for the following day. She set them for the morning so she could get lunch with Ginny after. She sent a quick text to Ginny to tell her she could do lunch tomorrow.

Josh called to let her know he was going to the JL13 office to collect some files. Having nothing in particular to do, she decided to go to her mum and dad's. Ava and Derek would be at work, so she was hoping to get the chance to speak with her parents alone.

She knocked loudly on their door and waited patiently for them to answer. Her dad did so, and she entered giving him a hug.

'Your mother is out doing the food shopping,' he told her. 'What are you doing at home at this time of day?'

He had forgotten she quit her job on Monday. She reminded him, and asked how her mum was last night after they left.

'She was furious with Ella. Some of the things I heard her say were totally unacceptable,' he said. 'How are you feeling?' he asked, and she could see concern etched across his face.

'I'm fine. My extreme emotion bucket was already full to the brim by the time I got here yesterday evening. I did feel very sorry for Casey. That was until he called me earlier to ask me what I said to provoke her.'

'He did not.' Mr Cooper looked pissed. 'What did you say?'

'I told him to call me back once he'd had the chance to reflect on what he was asking me.'

'Good,' he said. 'I know that he is in a bit of a predicament with her being his wife and all, but there is no defending her behaviour. It's disrespectful.'

Danielle wholeheartedly agreed. She didn't think Ava was changing her mind about letting her in the house again any time soon either.

Her dad made them an Irish coffee and they sat outside under the parasol drinking and chatting. She loved her dad so much. He was such a family man. All four of his children were grown, and yet, since the day they were born, his kids were his primary focus.

Danielle felt so lucky to have the family she had around her. She was sure her confidence and personality, stemmed from having such a secure home environment growing up. She always felt protected and loved.

She told her dad about the voicemail from Aimee and asked his advice. He told her to do nothing. To ignore it and stay silent. Danielle felt assured that she had done the right thing. She just hoped that Josh had forgotten about it and didn't react.

The garden clock told her it was quarter to four. She had completely lost track of time. Her mum had returned from shopping and joined them in the garden. Danielle didn't want to keep them any longer, and wasn't sure what time Josh was getting back. She said her goodbyes and made her way back home.

When she got back, she found Josh sitting on the doorstep waiting for her. He stood up when she came down the path towards him.

'Sorry. I didn't know what time you would be finished. I need to get you a key...' she was silenced by the long, hard kiss he planted on her.

'Hello baby,' he said, and she felt her knees weaken.

They went inside and were lazing on the sofa, entwined and at ease. He had asked her to read the sales report he had been given by Lucy. He didn't really understand what it meant, so asked for her analysis. She thought he may have more than one objective when handing the report to her. She kept quiet. That conversation was a nonstarter, so there would be no point in bringing it up.

She leaned forward to grab a pen from the coffee table, and started circling figures and jotting a few notes. Josh was watching her with a grin that told her he thought his plan was working.

'There are a few things you need to ask for,' she said, sitting up to face him. 'These sales figures don't make sense.'

She went on to explain why the figures were off. She told him to ask for a breakdown by hour for the eleven days JL13 had been trading. She also told him to get a report on website traffic, broken down by time. She had a feeling that there was an issue with the website at certain times of the day.

He looked at her, baffled. She rolled her eyes and asked him for his phone so she could compose the email. She sent it off and asked Lucy to get this information by lunch time tomorrow.

'Wow. I'm so assertive,' he said, reading over her shoulder.

'This is a big deal Josh,' she retorted. 'These figures are not matching the forecast, and you need to make sense of it.'

She sent a second email to Jarrod to ask him to review the social media activity. She wanted to see if anyone had commented on the speed of the website, or if any crashes were reported.

'I think I quite like having a secretary.' He smiled and moved her hair out of the way so he could kiss her neck.

'You'd better get recruiting then because I ain't no secretary,' she responded.

He stuck out his bottom lip to convey mock sadness. She leaned in close and bit the lip playfully.

Josh masterfully undressed her with his one functional hand until she was completely naked. He teased her relentlessly, driving her to the brink of orgasm and stopping. His hands and mouth were working expertly. It was as if he knew exactly how her body would respond to his touch.

She was so hot and frustrated, she begged him to let her come. She had no shame. Her only thoughts were taken up by finding a way to get him inside her.

Josh must have been aware that she was nearing the edge of despair, because it was at that moment he freed his cock, and plunged himself inside her.

Danielle made noises she had never heard herself make before. The power of her orgasm was overwhelming. She was so raw, so on edge, so desperate. Her every nerve tingled as her body thrashed and spasmed in response to him. He cupped her arse to adjust her pelvis giving him more access to her quivering sex. He drove inside of her with perfectly precise thrusts, until she orgasmed a second time.

Feeling her tighten around him as she squealed in pleasure, sent him in to a spin. He quickened his pace. She was bucking up and into him, wanting to get as close as possible. Josh came hard. His eyes rolled in to the back of his head as she held on to him.

Danielle insisted they shower separately, as she didn't think she could take anymore at that moment. They returned to the lounge one at a time. They ordered pizza and watched a quiz show. She was delightfully taken aback when he shouted out the correct answers to a few of the questions. She really had stereotyped him as a dumb footballer.

They sat comfortably exchanging stories about their lives as they ate pizza. Danielle was pleased that they could sit and talk, without the constant need to jump each other's bones.

Halfway through a slice of ham and pineapple, she remembered she hadn't asked him about his physio. She covered her half full mouth with her hand, and asked him.

He told her that he had been given exercises to do daily to regain dexterity. His manager, after consulting the doctors, confirmed that he would be training in the gym with an assigned personal trainer to maintain muscle mass. This would continue for two weeks, and they then would review with the intention of getting him back to cardio. Depending on how well the fracture healed, he could be ready to start full training, and be fit to play in five weeks.

Danielle decided not to ask him about his ongoing plans for his sleeping arrangements. She didn't want to hear him say what she already knew, that he needed to be closer to the training ground.

'I'm going into town tomorrow. I have two meetings with potential clients, and then I'm meeting Ginny for lunch.'

He stopped the slice of pizza he had in his hand from reaching his mouth, and set it back down on the box.

'Are you seriously telling me you're going to speak to other companies and aren't coming back to work with me? I need you.'

His face had turned serious and angry. She was startled by the change in the atmosphere. He was looking at her with an expression she had never seen before.

'I told you, I'm not coming back. It was too much when I originally quit. Now, working there would be a complete clusterfuck,' she said softly. She was trying to pacify him without backing down.

'I can't believe you would be so unprofessional,' he said.

'Excuse me?'

'You made a commitment when you signed your contract, and I expect you to keep it.'

Danielle couldn't believe that he would speak to her this way. She pointed out that this argument, and his attitude change towards her, was exactly the reason she couldn't work with him.

'You are out of order,' he said.

'You might want to take some time to rethink how you speak to me because if you continue like this, it won't just be the job I walk away from.' Danielle had seen red. She reacted without thinking.

'How dare you threaten me with that.'

He took out his phone and fired off a message. He was sending for a driver to come and pick him up. He kept his head down and wouldn't look at her. She knew she had gone too far. She wanted to push a reaction out of him because she was angry.

Too stubborn to say anything to stop him, she watched on silently as he gathered his things, and left.

Chapter 28

Danielle went to bed that evening, and woke up the following morning, alone. She kept checking her phone throughout the night to see if he had text, but he hadn't. She decided that she was not entirely at fault. He wasn't listening. She told him multiple times she wasn't going back, and he had just ignored her, and pushed his own agenda. That wasn't fair. He may be used to getting his own way, but knew by now that it wouldn't be that way with her.

She dressed in a long sleeve cream blouse that tied at the neck. The sleeves had ruffled edging, and the material was light. She paired this with a plain grey skirt that ended halfway down her thigh. She finished the outfit with her trademark black tights, and a pair of grey, round toed heels with a buckled strap. She wore her dark hair down, and added a grey head band to pull her hair away from her face. She applied some light foundation and blackened her eyelashes with mascara. Finally, she added some small, hooped silver earrings and her Rolex her parents got her on her 30th birthday. The watch was engraved at the back with a cute message wishing her a happy birthday. She checked her final look in the mirror, grabbed her bag, and made her way to the train station.

Her first meeting went well. She met with the managing director and owner of a Lloyd's syndicate. They had been given capacity to expand their portfolio, and were looking for someone to help them break into a new market. Danielle explained her methods, and what she expected as a fee. She left the coffee shop they had met in, confident that they would be her next project.

The second meeting was a disappointment. Their initial contact implied they had secured the funds to launch a chain of vegan restaurants. When she probed a little deeper, they revealed that they were still missing twenty two percent of the startup capital needed. She thanked them for their time, and advised that the project wouldn't be for her. She hated being lied to, and she hated time wasters even more. She made a mental note to add another question in to her prospectus format and headed off to meet Ginny.

She got to the Gaucho fifteen minutes earlier than the scheduled meeting time. She thought her previous meeting would have lasted longer, but had to cut it short. She was shown to her seat in the main restaurant and ordered a bottle of Argentinian red wine. She and Ginny had shared this bottle before, so she knew she would approve.

The waiter was pouring her a glass when Ginny came bursting in like a whirlwind. Danielle thanked the waiter and pointed at the empty glass in front of Ginny, signalling him to fill that glass too.

No sooner than her arse hit the cow Hyde chair, did Ginny launch into a whole story about what was happening with George, the man she had spent the night with after the launch event. Danielle sent the waiter away twice because they hadn't yet opened the menu.

Danielle seized on the advantage to talk when Ginny took a gulp of her wine, to ask her if she knew what she wanted to eat.

'Oh yeah, I have the same every time. Eight-ounce ribeye, medium with fries and side of green beans and creamed spinach.'

Danielle rolled her eyes, thinking that they could have ordered much earlier, and called the waiter over advising they were finally ready. She put her hand up to stop Ginny from talking again before the waiter had reached their table. When he arrived, she ordered both of their meals as Danielle wanted the same. When the waiter stepped away from the table, she dropped her halting hand, and Ginny resumed her animation.

'How's work been the last few days?' Danielle asked cautiously. She knew Ginny was still mad at her for suddenly bailing, and didn't want another earful.

'Ok. Lucy is running round like a headless chicken without you. You could have done a handover,' she said, looking pointedly at her friend.

'I put one together last night and sent it over this morning.'

'Oh,' Ginny said. Danielle had clearly taken the wind out of her sails on that one. She followed up with, 'I'm surprised you had the time to do that. I thought you and Mr Smarm would be shagging constantly.'

Danielle told her about Josh walking out, and that she hadn't heard from him since. She felt a pang of sadness as she said it out loud for the first time.

'Did you really need to threaten him with that Dan?' Ginny said. 'It's a bit OTT don't you think?'

'I was just so angry that he thought I was obliged to do what he said. So, I lashed out.'

'Technically he could make you come in. Your contract does have a week's notice period-built in.'

'I know,' she said.

They paused whilst two waiters laid food in front of each of them. One of them remained to top up their glasses and then retreated.

'He didn't need to walk out though. That was childish,' Ginny said. 'That explains his mood in the office this morning. He was a miserable fuck.'

They ate and finished the bottle. Ginny advised she needed to get back to the office, and stood up to say goodbye to Danielle. Her phone buzzed before she reached her. Ginny looked at it and saw she had a message from Josh. She read it, then held up the phone for Danielle.

*'Take the rest of the day. I know you ladies will have a lot to talk about.'*

Ginny didn't need telling twice. She called to the waiter and signalled that they would have another bottle.

## Chapter 29

They had such a great afternoon that Danielle had almost forgotten about her Josh issue. They had drinks in a number of bars, and Danielle found herself drunk for the first time in years. They bumped into a couple of Danielle's old work colleagues in Leadenhall market, and sat with them drinking and catching up. Unbeknownst to Danielle, Ginny had been taking pictures all afternoon and evening, and posting them to her Facebook and Instagram accounts.

She was in the toilet cubicle when she heard heavy footsteps, followed by Josh shouting her name. He must have seen the pictures.

'Danielle,' he said again. 'Fucking answer me, now.'

'I'm peeing at the moment,' she said, laughing.

She was leaning her head on the toilet roll holder. She forced herself to keep her eyes open, because she knew she would fall asleep if they closed.

She was finding it impossible to pull up her tights and reposition her skirt. Josh knocked on her door and demanded she open it.

'Stop bossing me around,' she slurred, but she unlocked the door.

'Jesus!' he said. He took over redressing her and she let him. 'Why are you so mangled? It's dangerous to be this drunk around here. And who the fuck are those guys you are with?'

'Why do you care?' she answered, looking at him defiantly.

'For fucks sake Danielle. What sort of a question is that?' He ran his hands through his hair, exasperated.

He looked so gorgeous when he did that.

'You. Are so. Handsome.' She flung her arms round his neck and kissed him.

He didn't stop her. His body took over his rational mind in the same way hers did. He lifted her up on to the sink and stood between her legs. He deepened the kiss, and she pulled herself closer so she could grab his arse. Her hand moved around to the front, when he stopped abruptly, and pulled away.

'I'm not fucking you in the toilet of some dirty pub,' he said.

'Why not?' She was pouting.

'Because it's filthy, anyone could walk in, and when you are sober you will kill me.'

'I won't,' she said, raising her chin in defiance.

'Come on. I'm taking you home.'

He escorted her back to the table and told Ginny it was time to go. The look on his face was such that even *she*, didn't test him on it.

'They're fine to stay. They wanna try an arsenal man.' One of her old colleagues decided to challenge.

'Fuck off mate. I'm not in the mood for jumped up pricks right now.' Josh turned, and ushered the girls away and into the car that was idling outside.

Danielle was hungover for three days. She barely left her bed. Josh came back each afternoon and took care of her. She was so embarrassed but powerless to do anything about it. Surely, he was put off by the state of her.

It was Saturday before she felt normal again. She took a long shower and scrubbed herself clean of three days' worth of scum. She washed her hair twice to make sure she was fresh and clean. She stripped the bed and put the items in the wash. She was making herself a cup of coffee when Josh came in using her key.

She ran to him and gave him a big hug, thanking him for looking after her, and apologising for the state she got herself in. He didn't hug her back. She took a step back and looked at him confused. He was rooted to the spot avoiding her eyes.

She recoiled further hugging herself. Something was really wrong. Was he that disgusted by her when she lay in the bed recovering from her hangover? Had he decided that she wasn't for him after all? These thoughts plagued her mind, but she waved them away. No. Their connection was deeper than the superficial. They were absolutely in love with each other, whether they had said the words or not.

'Tell me what's wrong,' she said, choking the words out.

He stayed silent for what felt like an eternity. Eventually, he showed her the picture on his phone. It was a scan picture with the words, 'baby Linberg' in the top right-hand corner.

'Aimee's three months pregnant.'

Printed in Great Britain
by Amazon

56935500R00139